the DEMON in him

AN UNEARTHLY SINS NOVEL

Stefanie Dawn

The Demon in Him
An Unearthly Sins Novel

Stefanie Dawn

ISBN: 978-1763870468

Editing and Proofing by Swish Design & Editing
Book Design by Swish Design & Editing
Cover Design by Opium House Creatives
Published by Angels and Fire Books
Cover Image Copyright 2023

DEDICATION

To all the characters in the *Unearthly Sins* novels,
I'm thankful you'll live on in my mind.
Otherwise, I'd miss you too much.

the DEMON in him

AN UNEARTHLY SINS NOVEL

CHAPTER
1

TATE

To sever a mated bond between demons, they must endure pain to their breaking point.

To sever a bond between a demon and a human, care must be taken to ensure the human—in this case, me—isn't killed in the process. Although not *too much* care. Demons don't take bonding lightly. A bonding was a deal, a promise, an oath, which, when broken, lowered demons in the eyes of others of their kind. Humans are already fairly low in the pecking order in the eyes of demons, and if it were possible for us to sink lower in their opinion, it would be if we broke a bond.

If the commitment couldn't be forever, then why make it in the first place? If it wasn't a commitment, then it was a fuck, and nothing else. A bond made between mates was one of blood and flesh, and destroying that was done only when there was no other option short of death.

So we must endure pain during the severing to remind us of the promise we were breaking.

Blood was given, and flesh will be taken.

Mike didn't want to kill me, and despite my now unbonded mate instigating the severing of the bond, just as he had instigated the bonding in the first place, I knew he still loved me in some way. But Mike was weak. He wasn't a true demon but a being denying his heritage, blood, and power.

And weakness could be exploited.

Did I ever love him? Maybe, in my own way. He was the family I never had, the one who tried to show me I was worthy of his love as he tried to see past the violent exterior that no one else bothered to explore. But I wasn't worthy, and Mike wanted me to change for him.

I never would.

As a human, I couldn't be dragged to Hell without being killed, and Hell was where a bonding was traditionally broken. So, compromises had to be made, and two demons came to Earth to sever our bond for us. The shame of breaking a bond meant it couldn't be done in private between the two parties. Others must be notified, and two other demons must drag us apart, physically and spiritually. Bindings of red, black, and gold glowed across our skin, wrapping around us and joining us together, already painful with the sting and burn as they gripped the skin of our naked bodies. Translucent ropes wove around our arms, torsos, and legs. Ropes of power and promise were achingly and slowly pulled off us while the correct incantations were spoken, leaving deep welts as they continued to scrape against our exposed flesh long after the top layers of skin were gone.

It was excruciating, and while I tried not to give the assisting demons the satisfaction of screaming, I couldn't hold it back. My throat was raw long before the ceremony was over, and I swore the cuts went down to the bone by the time it was finished. Mike would heal faster than me, and with the demon blood that ran through me since the bonding, I would heal faster than a normal human. But it would still take time and leave me with scars that would never fade. Wounds born of magic and demonic power were not the same as a simple cut or scrape.

I tried to remember back to before Mike and I bonded, and I don't think I ever wanted to take that step with him in the first place. But it was important to Mike—he said he loved me and wanted to show me how much. So I drank his blood from a cut made by his hand, and as the silky, warm liquid slid down my throat, my body revolted against the demonic power that threatened to overcome my humanity— what little humanity I had left. After the second session, we were bonded, and my lifespan was increased as I was interpolated with extra strength, speed, and power. My eyes would turn yellow when I was angry, emotional, or taking part in violence or sex, and after a while, I learned to control it.

But I wasn't a demon, only a bonded human. Mike was stronger than me, physically at least.

The power was intoxicating, and after a lifetime of being treated like scum, I wanted more. The demonic influence in my blood and body only enhanced the parts of me Mike had tried to pretend didn't exist—the lust for violence, the pleasure in others' pain, and the joy in taking down those weaker than me. There were always remaining questions I wanted to ask Mike. I wanted to know if he saw these things in me before the bonding and simply pretended they weren't there, or if he was so naïve that his love for me blinded him to what I truly was.

A monster.

A man with little to no morals and even less empathy. I wasn't ashamed of what I was, I was merely a product of my environment and genes, and I could spend a lifetime denying it or embrace it. The additional strength and yellow eyes were useful for intimidation, and I think it hurt Mike to know that I was more concerned with how these changes benefitted me than progressing our relationship.

Some demon he was. When he had told me of his hidden nature, of course, I didn't believe him, but then he showed me his true form, and I was beyond awed. He loved me, and with a demon on my side, perhaps my life would get better. Something tugged at my chest at the idea of being protected and having someone who was looking out for me simply because they cared. A foreign concept.

But Mike wanted what I couldn't offer—true love in return—and if I were born with the capability to love, it was long gone now. He wanted to turn his back on everything that made him the magnificent supernatural beast he was. Demons had urges—violence and sex—that, if denied, their body and inner demon would revolt against each other. Mike was determined. He wanted no violence and desired to be a true part of human society, and the more I tried to push him to join my family business—my father running one of the largest underground crime syndicates in the city—the more Mike resisted. He stopped giving into the urges, and our fucking became less violent until he was holding back to the point of being only gentle with me in bed.

I didn't want that. I wanted the demon I had met—the protective man and his possessiveness, who had lost control and taken me against the wall of his apartment after our second date. And yes, maybe I also wanted the kind and nurturing streak that had made me feel *something*, which was *something* more than I had felt in my life outside of anger and hatred. I wanted his power and the power that came with us as a unit once we bonded. I wanted us to be a team, for Mike to embrace his demon as I had mine long before I knew they were literal.

I wanted to use my new power to kill my father, to make him bleed, squirm, and feel all the pain I could inflict.

And my sister... I would do things to her that would make her wish she were dead.

Mike had told me about the rules governing demons—they couldn't kill humans without the consequence of being sent back to Hell with no option to return to Earth. However, I reminded him I wasn't a demon but a human with demon powers and wasn't subject to those rules.

After some months together, I'd tested out my new powers and abilities and found that violence brought with it a rush of pleasure that made my eyes flash and my muscles ripple as the demon blood merged with my own. There was some bullshit thing with a bond where, while we could have sex with other beings, it was physically painful, much as it was painful to be too far from our mate. So the woman I had cornered in a club and dragged out back to my car, I wasn't able to fuck her in the back seat as I planned. But she was screaming and fighting me the whole way, and torturing her was sweet pleasure to me, dragging my teeth down her body until she bled and holding my father's gun between her legs, whispering threats that made her tremble with tears.

Exhilarating.

I told Mike of my pleasures, and he looked at me as if he'd never seen me before. He didn't understand since bonded partners meant that being with someone else was painful, why I would even try. He asked, didn't I love him and only him? I had wondered what the pain was like of being with someone outside the bond and told him it had only added to my pleasure.

Although he tried for a short while longer to find something pure inside me that wasn't there, that was the beginning of the end for us.

Pity, I enjoyed the sex.

CHAPTER
2

MIKE

Raising my hands in surrender, I slowly approached the demon in front of me.

Frank, in his human form, was an attractive man, and he knew it. He'd spent his short time on Earth picking up women and partaking in one-night stands and group sex. I had no issue with that. As long as he wasn't hurting anyone or himself, he could do as he pleased while on the surface.

But not this.

The scent of blood was thick in the air between us. I could practically hear it swirling around his tongue as he lapped at the wound on the young woman's neck. Her chin rested on his shoulder as his mouth was buried in the crook of her neck, bent over her as she sprawled on the floor, the sounds from the house party downstairs partially blocked out by the closed door. Her eyes were glazed in ecstasy while Frank worked his hand between her legs, the exact nature of his motion obscured by her skirt.

But Frank was barely paying attention to his hand or what he was doing, running purely on instinct to bring her pleasure. Because at this point, he was already lost to the drug that is human blood, and if he didn't stop soon, he could kill her.

Unacceptable.

He wouldn't want to hurt a human, not if he was in complete control. But Frank was beyond that point, his eyes yellow with black slits for irises, and where his other hand gripped her throat, his fingers were elongating and graying at the tips as his natural color took over them, cracking as they extended. Too many joints to be human. Whether the woman realized she was doing it or not, one hand was weakly batting against Frank's chest. Somewhere inside, she could feel herself growing weaker, her body running on instinct and telling her she was losing too much blood, even if her mind hadn't caught up yet.

"Frank," I spoke gently so as not to startle him. This close to transforming back into his demon form, he could shred her throat before he realized

he had moved. He was younger than me, new to Earth, and hadn't yet learned complete control. "Let her go... you've had enough."

Frank pulled away from her neck with a long hiss through his teeth. He moved away just enough to talk to me but continued to dip his tongue against the wound on her throat. Humming with satisfaction, he whispered, "But she loves it."

She had closed her eyes and tilted her head back, bucking her hips against his busy hand. "Yes..." she mumbled.

A moan rumbled through Frank's chest as he watched her, his yellow eyes glowing. "And she's about to come. Aren't you, my sweet toy?" Those final words were whispered against her ear as she moaned, and he moved to bring his lips back to her neck.

"Frank." This time I used force in my voice, edged with a warning before he could take more blood. "You could kill her."

"I know what I'm doing." He threw me a look of such hatred that if I didn't know him, I would've recoiled from it. Right now, he was an embodiment of everything I hated about demons, taking what they wanted when they wanted, giving in to their desires for violence and sex. I had known Frank for a long time, even if it was distantly, and I could help him if only he would let the girl go.

"No." I'd had enough, and I stepped forward, grabbing his shoulder. "You fucking don't know what you're doing." Frank snarled at me as I yanked at his shoulder. Grabbing the back of his head, I pushed his face against my chest as the woman opened her eyes. She didn't need a glimpse of the demon who had just been feasting on her blood. Frank struggled against my grip, and I could barely contain him. This close to the change, Frank's strength was increased.

But I was older, more controlled, and could contain him.

For now.

"Let me finish!" He snarled.

"You don't want to kill her," I hissed against his ear, watching as the woman came out of her pleasured daze.

"I wasn't going to."

Relief flooded me at this, not because of his words, but that his tone had lost the ethereal edge to it. He was regaining control. Slowly.

The woman tried to lift herself into a sitting position, bringing a hand to her head as her vision swam before she dropped back to the floor.

"Stay where you are," I told her.

She looked at me, blinking lazily. "Why am I so weak?"

"Must've been something you drank."

Frank chuckled darkly against my chest, and I

increased my grip on his hair, twisting his dark curls in my fist. She didn't need to know how close she was to losing consciousness due to blood loss. Left alone with Frank, if he had lost control, I feared he would have drained her life.

"You have a lot to learn," I murmured in Frank's ear. He was still struggling against my hold, although his efforts were steadily decreasing. "I can help you."

"I don't need your help."

"You must stop drinking blood. It's the worst kind of drug."

Frank tore himself from my grip, grabbed my forearms and snarled at me, ending with a smirk. "It's the best *kind of drug, and I'll keep taking it because these women come* so fucking hard *when I drink their blood at the same time."*

Frowning, I glanced over his shoulder, spinning Frank to face the unconscious woman on the floor. "Get your shit together, Frank. Look at her! She's fucking *unconscious. If you had kept going, you could have killed her. She needs a hospital. Now."*

Frank shook his head as if shaking away the thoughts before running his hands over his face. His skin was shifting back to human tone, and I sighed quietly as he blinked rapidly, each time the yellow tint clearing more. He was regaining control at the same time the reality of his actions set in.

"Fuck," he mumbled, punching the wall for emphasis and knocking a fist-sized hole in it. "Fuck!"

Without waiting for him to finish his epiphany, I gripped his arm, checking briefly to make sure his eyes had returned to brown, and dragged him from the room, thankful for the darkness in the hall to cover the blood stains on the front of his shirt. Once downstairs, I found the nearest woman who looked to be the same age as the woman Frank had been with and told her to call an ambulance. She was on her cell even as she ran upstairs.

Shoving Frank out the front door, I didn't let go of my grip on his arm until I pushed him into the passenger seat of my car.

"All right, Mike. I got it already. I fucked up."

"You could've killed her, Frank."

"You said that already." He huffed.

"Because it's fucking important."

I slammed the door before he could respond, moving around the vehicle to get into the driver's seat. I knew Frank, and he was still young.

He had a lot to learn, but I could help him.

"I've fucking *got it!*" Frank slammed his palm on my desk as he strolled past, and I jumped slightly in my chair, watching as Frank's swagger filled with an extra dose of smugness as though every one of his ideas was gold. He turned back to me. "Are you even paying attention?"

I shook the thoughts from my head, correlating the image of the demon in front of me with the demon in my memory. Frank had come a long way since those days. He was controlled now, and although he used his natural charm more than I'd like him to, he was trustworthy.

Even if he was arrogant as fuck.

"Sorry, was just thinking about when we met properly for the first time."

Frank's lip curled in distaste. "Why?"

I shrugged. "I don't know. Just this talk about expanding the business made me think of the early days."

"Well, that's a nice trip down memory lane and all, but I don't need the reminder." He made a point of glancing at my wrists. Even though my sleeves were pulled down and the scars from my severed bonding were not visible, his point was clear. "You understand, right?"

Sneering at him, I couldn't help the subconscious rub of my wrists and readjustment of my sleeves.

Our architecture firm had been steadily expanding for almost a decade, really kicking off when we moved into our new offices around six years ago. Now, we were looking at next-level expansion—a new branch interstate. But the question was, where would be the best place to start?

"Do tell your wonderful idea," I muttered, kicking my feet up on my desk and tilting my chair back, the pen I had been jotting notes down with tapping against my jaw.

"Miami Beach." Frank's grin was triumphant. His chin tilted slightly upward as if saying *I know I'm a genius, and I'm ready for your applause now.*

Smirking, I regarded the younger demon in front of me. Just under two decades ago, I'd decided to bring him on board at my business, which at that time was only me, alone, running off a laptop out of my small apartment. Frank wasn't overly pleased I'd insisted he get the correct education first, as diplomas in business, accounting, and architecture were a must as far as I was concerned. I'd done it right, and I expected the same from him. If he wanted to live on Earth with me, as a human, then we would do things correctly by the rules of this world, and while demons could be incredibly persuasive through charm and intimidation, I'd never used those abilities to gain my position.

Frank had but only a little.

Probably more than he'd admitted to me.

He'd made a formidable business partner with his savvy, ideas, and willingness to charm the right people. We'd been launched into the public scene after a few choice clients were thrilled with our designs.

Where do *you get your inspiration from?*

My smirk faltered slightly, for the clean lines and gothic undertones were an adaptation from home.

Hell.

I was coming up on over twenty years on Earth myself, and thankfully, my hair had grayed with time, for otherwise, I would look much too young to be in the position I was. I imagine if I was as public as Frank was, plastering my face in articles and promotional materials, I'd be accused of using Botox, at the very least. I told people I was in my fifties, but the reality was far beyond that.

When my hair started to gray, I let it, and Frank would run his fingers through his dark, curly hair and tell me I was the *sophisticated one.* I'd ask what that made him, and he'd reply the *moneymaker.*

Cheeky asshole.

Frank waited for my praise for his most recent idea, but I wasn't feeling it. The legs of my chair hit the carpet with a dulled thunk as I tilted the chair forward before resting my elbows on the desk. "I'm not sure Florida is the place for our business. Keeping in mind one of us would have to relocate, temporarily at least, to get it up and running, and I'm sure as hell am not keen on living there."

"I'll go," Frank offered, dropping into the chair on the other side of my expansive desk.

"Oh really?" I raised my eyebrows at him. "And Charlotte would be happy to uproot her career and go with you, I suppose?" While I ended on an inflection, it was a rhetorical question. Charlotte—Frank's bonded mate, a human—was career-driven, and in the past three years since she worked as Frank's assistant who subsequently fell in love with him—she'd worked hard to build a career as an architect. Frank knew as well as I she wouldn't want to move, although she would if it meant that much to him. Frank was an asshole, but he loved her, and he wouldn't want her upset.

"Fine." Frank slumped back in the chair, lifting his feet onto my desk as I had done.

"Move them," I snapped. It was my desk, and only I was allowed to put my feet on it. Besides, Frank was always issuing tiny challenges to my authority, and if I let even one of them slide, he would take a mile. He'd never screw me over—we worked too well together—but at the end of the day, demons were demons, and every struggle was one of power and territory.

He did as told with a sly look before sighing loudly and linking his fingers behind his head. "Where do *you* want to go then?"

"It's not where *I* want to go but where it will be good for business." I adjusted my tie, loosening the knot. "I'm thinking San Francisco or Chicago."

Frank pretended to consider my suggestions,

tapping his chin in an obvious attempt to mock me. I raised a brow at him, knowing he was baiting me, as he often did. Frank was adamant that I didn't let my demon desires out often enough, and he was probably right. A few years ago, it had resulted in a loss of control that spelled absolute disaster I try not to think about. Every now and then, Frank did the psychological equivalent of poking me with a sharp stick to ensure I had everything under control. He also didn't approve of the method I'd chosen over two decades ago to keep myself in control, stating that demons simply had to fuck and fight. But I disagreed, and apart from one incident, I'd been fine for my entire life on Earth.

Demons denied of their urges on Earth would turn into less than animals—a bundle of rage and desire—turning into our true forms and taking control. It ended up messy, so all demons who came to Earth knew they needed to give into their desires for violence and sex, lest they be forced to by losing control.

In saying that, demons didn't usually stay on Earth as long as we had. I had well and truly turned my back on my heritage. Frank liked to play the line between the two.

But he was good at it, and I trusted him to maintain control.

"Well," he said, slapping his palms on his knees. "Plan your arguments for later because I've got another meeting to go to."

Standing to meet Frank before he reached the door, I slapped a palm against his chest. His lip lifted in irritation, and I smiled an easy, lazy smile that spoke of power. No matter how much I denied my demon, we knew if I wanted to call on that power, it was there, and I was older than Frank. Faster.

Although history had taught me he was stronger. Physically, he was bigger than me, despite being the same height. He also had years of fighting experience on me, years when I'd been busy finding other avenues to control my demon short of getting together with a group of demons and tearing each other apart.

There was a reason I left Hell, and mindless violence for the sake of it was one of them. But a few years ago, I had lost control, and my demon had taken over, almost forcing a full transformation before causing some serious damage. To this day, I was unable to recall how I had gotten there, but I found myself in a drug lab in the middle of the countryside, hours outside the city and alone with questionable men. By that point, I was already beyond reproach.

While my memory of the event is hazy, I do recall coming to my senses, a little bit at least, and found myself standing in the middle of the room with the remains of the men strewn around me. I had to swallow back the lump in my throat, holding down the bile as I remembered the metallic tang of the blood across my tongue. I never wanted violence. I'd spent decades trying to escape it, but I had lost control in the worst possible way and killed human men. Whether or not they deserved it was irrelevant. It was not my place to make that call. Usually, a demon killing a human would result in banishment back to Hell, but there had been no consequences, and no one had come to find and drag me away kicking and screaming. There was nothing.

Frank suggested the death of those men was God's will, and I was nothing but a tool in the right place at the right time, exactly as I was meant to, to enact justice on men who deserved to die.

I didn't buy it, but since I couldn't think of another explanation, I said nothing.

Frank had taken me down that night. He had no choice, and although I couldn't forget the feel of my claws tearing through the skin on his chest and his return blows, I'd been thankful he'd been strong enough to do it. And I'm certain he enjoyed the part where he knocked me out before shoving me in the trunk of his car. That was probably revenge for me grabbing at Charlotte. They had already begun the bonding process at that stage, and he was so possessive over her I'm surprised he didn't kill me when I dared to touch her in my animalistic state.

Since then, I'd begrudgingly taken part in the

fight club on the rare occasion my usual method of control wasn't cutting it. There were two things a demon craved—fucking and fighting—and denied those on Earth would result in a loss of control while our instinct searched for what it craved, relentlessly and dangerously.

So control was essential.

My fighting skill had improved, and recently I'd bested Frank. These tiny rebellions of his within the business were his way of trying to regain some of the control he'd lost during the fight. The dominance that ran so thick through him had been challenged, and I was the challenger.

In his mind, at least.

Here I was a co-CEO, the boss, the *man*, but I also wasn't going to tolerate his fits, and if I had to take him down in the office right here, I would. Sworn off violence or not, this business was mine, and I'd protect it.

"Correction," I drawled, patting his chest lightly before withdrawing my hand, "*I* have another meeting to go to."

"I thought we were meeting with the Macintyre clan for their new project?"

"*I'm* meeting Mr. Macintyre, he's one of our biggest clients, who I handle personally. *You* need to go deal with the Wilson account."

Frank's lip turned up, somewhere between a sneer and a snarl. "I can't stand that woman."

Laughing, I clapped Frank's shoulder, his muscles tensing in irritation. "Oh, come on, use your world-famous charm."

"Yeah, right. My balls shrivel up and disappear when she comes near me."

"Come now, she's pretty and just your type."

"Even before I was bonded to Charlotte, *Mrs.* Wilson's looks did little to quell my dislike for her. She always looks like something smells bad and treats me like your lackey."

"You *are* my—"

A true growl filtered through Frank's throat then. "Don't say it, don't you dare. We're partners."

I chuckled. "Yes, we are. I'm just stirring you up."

"And it's working."

"I know," I said, grabbing my jacket and briefcase. "It always does."

Before the business meeting, I had a stop to make, and while there would be no real harm in Frank being in on the Macintyre account, I didn't want him present for the more personal business I had to take care of.

The metal of the chair legs scraped against the

pavers on the side street pathway, drawing the attention of the man already seated opposite me and the waitress inside. Sliding into my chair, I smirked as the man continued to look down at his hands folded on the table, the slightest twitch of his ears betraying him. He would have heard I was close long before he saw me round the corner.

Werewolves' hearing was impeccable, even in human form.

Dante kept his black hair around shoulder length, constantly looking as though it were in need of a good comb. His hands were tanned and calloused, the hands of a working man, and they folded over each other, never quite motionless even as he mumbled his coffee order to the waitress when she approached. I was about to wave my hand to dismiss her when Dante grunted, and I took that to mean he had something to discuss with me beyond a friendly check-up, so I ordered myself a coffee. Black, extra-large.

Friendly check-ups weren't exactly Dante's style anyway.

His green eyes were blazing when he met mine, and he said nothing until our order had been delivered and the waitress had left us alone. It was an awkward time, after the morning rush and before the lunch hour, and we were alone at the tables outside.

"There's trouble within the pack," he grunted

out, grabbing his coffee and taking a large gulp without waiting for it to cool. "You're no longer welcome."

While my hand stilled, paused in the movement between the table and my lips to taste my coffee, I moved past the moment of distraction and sipped delicately at my drink before returning it to the table, the mug clunking loudly against the glass after a slip of my control. He used the word *pack*, but werewolves were solitary creatures and very rare. They came together once a month if they could, to let off some steam and for tradition, I supposed, although the full moon had no effect on them. Perhaps it made them feel like they weren't so alone in the world, but at all other times, they moved and lived alone, staying apart from other weres and humans alike.

"Why?" I asked.

Dante looked at me and held my eye contact for a beat before he rolled his gaze away from mine and surveyed the street. His movements were rarely calm, always looking and listening at what was happening around him, his ears and nostrils twitching with movement that wouldn't be noticeable if I weren't looking for it. In its own way, a wolf-like motion.

I knew my scent bothered him. Werewolves and demons were natural enemies, but Dante and I had an understanding—a truce.

At least, that's what I thought. Apparently, things were changing.

"New members." His smile was cold, and we both knew what those people had gone through to become members. "They do not want to be associated with a group that hangs around a demon, even if it is for..." he traced his tongue around his lips, a hint of amusement in his eyes before it passed, "... therapy."

Despite popular belief, werewolves could not be created through the bite of another. It wasn't a curse passed down through generations, nor a fable told to children to keep them out of the woods at night. A human could not be turned into a were by an existing werewolf, and they didn't attack humans anyway.

A werewolf was a soldier of God, a human cursed to live out the remainder of their days until death with the were curse. But it was a saving grace, a small price to pay to avoid an eternity in Hell. A human who had not earned their place in Heaven but cemented their place in Hell could be offered a chance for redemption by an angel. If the angel saw something in them, perhaps a small spark worth saving, they could accept the curse of the werewolf, their soul would be redeemed, and they would be spared from an eternity in Hell.

Werewolves went by another name in popular lore.

Hellhounds.

They served a dual purpose on Earth. They were used to track down human souls that wouldn't cross over and demons who refused to play by the rules and drag them both back to Hell. When demons didn't want to get involved with their own kind or take the time to track one who was doing the wrong thing, a were could be called to do the job for them. It was a brutal act for a demon to be taken down by a werewolf. A demon would simply drag you through the gates of Hell, whereas a were would send you there by killing you and destroying your mark at the same time, so you could never return to Earth from Hell.

After my loss of control a few years ago when humans were killed and my skin was stained with blood, I was surprised the weres didn't come for me.

There were cities like this one where the demon population was so rampant that werewolves no longer lived within the city limits. But they weren't far, and when they were needed, they'd receive the call, a voice in their head telling them where to go, and they'd change form and track down their prey—the scent filling their nostrils, ready to be followed.

I often wondered what Dante had done to be offered the curse as a form of redemption, but it was not my place to ask, and he had never told me.

By instinct and law, weres and demons were enemies. But I had been allowed to be around them to enact my therapy to keep my demon under control, and it was only through an act of submission that I hadn't been killed when I first approached the pack.

But it seems those days were over.

"I understand you were taking a risk, even allowing me to be within the pack for those nights once a month." My mouth was dry, and I attempted to swallow but found nothing, so I took another sip of coffee. I was barely keeping my hand from trembling. The idea of losing the one outlet I was comfortable with to keep my demon under control would force me to take part in more traditional outlets. I would need to fight more often—something Frank would be happy about—but it meant giving into the violent nature I had tried so hard for so many years to deny. The denial of which I had down to a fine art, yet I felt it was teetering on the edge of taking control of me again. I had been so used to my pattern that to change it could have devastating effects.

I would also need to fuck more, something I craved to the point where I could almost feel the blood pulsing through my cock when I saw a human who aroused me, but again, I denied myself the temptation.

Mostly, the exceptionally rare one-night stand

was required.

I didn't want to risk losing control and hurt anyone.

Clearing my throat, I pulled my sleeves down to cover my wrists. Dante's eyes followed the movement, and his expression softened. He knew I was covering the scars, scars that can only be left from a severed bonding.

"You have to understand I need the outlet," I pleaded, but Dante was already leaning back in his chair, subconsciously removing himself from the conversation.

"I'm sorry," he said, standing before finishing his coffee. "It's not only my decision."

He left before I could argue, but I wasn't sure if I had the words to say anything anyway.

CHAPTER
3

JACOB

Every time I stepped into my father's office, it was a reminder that he expected me to be seated behind that desk one day. Graduating with a business degree under my belt, majoring in finance, my photograph was right on his desk, angled slightly toward the door so it couldn't be missed by anyone coming into his office. *My son, my pride and joy.*

And how could I let him down when he was so proud?

Timothy Macintyre, city planner working directly under the mayor, he liked to remind me that the city manager position would be coming available when Richard retired, and Dad *knew* people, so he could get in a good word for me. He was an honest man, and every smile I plastered on when we would talk about my future grated against me internally, much as my teeth ground together.

How could I tell him I had no interest in his business?

After school, I had done the degree simply because I didn't know what else to do, and while I was adept at what I did and had worked as an accountant since, it was hardly something I was passionate about. Whenever Dad would have meetings that he felt were *exciting* enough to draw me into his work, he would invite me along under the guise of having an outside opinion on the financials. But the not-so-sly smiles he threw me weren't fooling anyone.

Dammit, I wanted to make him proud.

But this life wasn't for me.

Wasn't that such a cliché? Wealthy family, only son who didn't want to follow in his father's footsteps and would ultimately let him down when he left town to *follow his dreams*. But it was a cliché I lived and breathed. My sisters had pursued their own career paths with little interference from Dad, but equal pride, and now he had a lawyer and a fashion designer. Their graduation pictures were displayed in his office too, but not pointed at the door.

Woe is me, right? I had no reason to complain, but every time I nodded and smiled at our weekly family dinner, telling Dad I'd love to come to his meetings, tours, or events was one more lie piled on top of the others, and eventually, it was going to break me.

Because in the garage I had rented out, separate from my small city loft apartment, was a convertible 1957 Ford T-Bird, and in my opinion, the sexiest fucking vehicle to ever exist. With a 312-V8 and over two hundred and forty horsepower behind it, I had actually down-sized the engine after discovering it would set off every car alarm in an underground parking lot if left to idle. While entertaining, it wasn't what I needed. It was a cruiser, and I wasn't out to make a statement—my car was for me only. Painted a deep green with ivory interior, the '57 was the last year of release before they redesigned the line, and as far as I'm concerned, ruined the sleek appearance of the bird.

Thanks to the elderly gentleman who lived next door when I was growing up, John was pivotal in my passion for cars. He was Italian, had a thick accent, and was a mechanic from the *old days* as he called them. He would roll up his shirt sleeves, exposing the gray hair on his tanned arms and a handful of tattoos that had faded and blurred with time, tilt his checkered cap to keep the sun from his eyes, and show me how to fix and maintain cars. Specializing, of course, in the classics, he wasn't bad when it came to new cars, but he didn't have the technology to hook them up and monitor the computer systems.

I didn't want to be sitting at a desk, dealing with accounts or architecture or the mayor's business, I wanted to be in the garage—*my* garage. I wanted to own the business, built purely on my knowledge of cars and the connections I'd made through years of side-project restorations, and share the passion with everyone who walked through the front doors.

But a mechanic wasn't a lawyer, a designer, a city planner, a doctor, or any other number of white-collar careers that would make my father swell with pride, hooking his thumbs in an almost comical fashion under his suspenders and bounce on his heels the way he did when he was particularly pleased.

Yet how long I could keep it a secret how miserable I was following this path was anyone's guess.

Mine would be not much longer at all, because the garage called to me, and I was at my most content with my head stuck under the propped-open hood of a classic car and my hands were caked with grease and grime.

Dad slapped me on the back as I strolled into his office. "Hope you don't mind giving up your lunch break to be here for this meeting." There was an almost permanent smile plastered on his face, and sometimes I wondered how much he knew about the city we lived in. Sure, it was fine *here*, but head south, and things got real dark, really quick. Crime was rampant, and it was no secret that the underground crime rings ran most of the city, including much of the police department, and how much they were in politics was anyone's guess. Yet here Dad was, working directly for the mayor with a constant smile, no worries in his eyes, and no cares beyond this office and the projects he had going.

I thought of my car and was at least thankful I could afford to keep her locked up at this end of the city, where she's safer.

"Not a problem, Dad," I said, returning his smile, albeit with less enthusiasm, and leaning against the edge of his desk. "What's the project this time?"

"Another apartment complex, closer to the restaurant district."

The restaurant district bordered between where the richest and poorest citizens lived. I wanted to ask him if such an apartment complex would have affordable rent to those south of the restaurant district. I didn't.

"Blackman, Conner, and Associates," Dad boomed, answering my unasked question of who the meeting was with today. Now that was a name I was familiar with. It was hard not to be. How many architecture firms do you know have billboards and plaster themselves across minor magazines as though they are some sort of B-grade celebrity? None I could think of, but it worked. The name came to mind almost straightaway when you thought of architecture, but I imagine that level of in-your-face advertising could only come from someone extremely arrogant.

And judging by what I'd seen of Frank Blackman, arrogance was one of his main traits—all dark hair and eyes and a grin that bordered on a smirk, promising that he'd take care of you in the business world.

And in the bedroom.

Shaking my head, I smirked to myself, and Dad returned the look with a smile, not knowing what was going on in my head. It's best he doesn't know. While Dad had no issue with my sexuality, I doubted he needed to know I was imagining getting fucked by the very architect he was looking to hire.

After a buzz from reception and an acknowledgment through the intercom from Dad, I pushed myself from the table and straightened, brushing my hands over my shirt and preparing to come face to face with the man from the magazines.

But when the door clicked open, it wasn't Frank standing there but his partner and co-CEO, Mike Conner.

And *fuck.*

While Mike was greeting my father, all easy smiles and firm handshakes, I gave myself a moment to trail my gaze over his body. It was near impossible to tell how old he was, only the silvering of his hair any indication of age, but his face was mostly line-free, and his shirt, while clearly expensive, fit around his arms, exposing a hint of some serious muscle. He looked like the sort who would leave his shirt unbuttoned a few at the top and sleeves rolled up to expose his forearms, which is one of the sexiest looks a man in a suit can have, by the way.

But maybe that was more Frank's deal because Mike's shirt was buttoned up to the neck, held in place with a navy tie, and his shirt was buttoned neatly at his wrists, with what looked like custom-engraved cufflinks glinting in the light as he shook Dad's hand.

My breath caught in my chest. I ground my teeth and stared at the ceiling for a moment, admonishing myself for looking at this man with anything other than a professional interest.

How long had it been since I'd been laid? Not that long, surely.

But then again, I'd recently restored the transmission on my Ford, not to mention rebuilding the engine, and I hadn't been out much during that time.

Damn. Okay, so it'd been a few months.

When I returned my gaze to the men greeting each other, I was startled to find Mike's eyes on mine, as though he'd been waiting for me to look back at him.

As though he could read my earlier thoughts.

Forcing control of myself so as not to blush like a schoolboy, I took a few purposeful steps forward and held out my hand. Mike took it without breaking eye contact and introduced himself. It was a beat too late before I realized I hadn't given him my name, and my father hastily introduced me to Mike. There was a presence about him that filled the room from the moment he stepped through the doors, and I couldn't drag my eyes from his, a deep stone-gray flecked with brown. Stunning. Despite his smirk, I refused to let myself be embarrassed at being unable to find the power to speak. He simply dominated the space between us and might as well have backed me against a wall and pressed his body to mine rather than shaking my hand with the way we were looking at each other.

I'm surprised literal sparks weren't coming off our hands.

Letting go of my hand, Mike nodded and smiled an award-winning smile, much like Frank's. But where Frank held confidence and arrogance, Mike was of sophistication. And perhaps, just below the surface, danger and possessiveness because I could absolutely picture those hands wrapping around my throat.

Fuck.

"Thank you for your time today," Mike said. He was directing the line at my father but hadn't taken his eyes from mine. I was the first to look away and added on a step backward, clearing the air around me of his intoxicating scent so I could at least concentrate.

"Of course, Mike, we've worked together before, so it's only fair we give you first crack at the new contract." With a wave of his hand, Dad guided Mike and me to sit at the small round table near the window, and as Mike unpacked his briefcase, Dad continued, "I hope you don't mind Jacob sitting in today. He's interested in coming into the family business as it were." He let go another chuckle, and I managed a weak smile, one that Mike did not return when he met my eyes, and the sound was sucked from my throat.

"I see," he crooned. Something in his face told me he knew I had *zero* interest in the family business, and while I wasn't a fan of being read so easily, I held his eye contact as long as I could. Mike continued, "It's not a problem at all. I'd be interested in his take on the design, since he's likely to have a fresher look."

Dad guffawed. "Kids these days, eh?"

I had no idea what he meant by that, and I arched an eyebrow at him, casting a sideways glance to see Mike chuckling under his breath politely. *Kids* seemed a bit of a stretch, but whatever. Businessmen were a breed of their own. You could say any old rubbish, and the other would be expected to laugh along, creating a false rapport that would come crashing down the second one of them left the building.

Unfolding several large sheets of paper on the table in front of us, Mike spun them around and using a pen, pointed out the features. As always, the interior had a hint of gothic architecture, while the outside was swept with clean lines—a perfect combination between functionality and aesthetic allure.

Dad was impressed, and given that his poker face was terrible, Mike must have known it. But there was no smug grin, simply the continued charisma of a businessman in his element. Watching his hands slide across the paperwork, his sleeve hitched up slightly to expose his wrist, and I frowned.

There's an extreme form of body augmentation called scarification, and while I'd never seen it in person, that's exactly what the marks on Mike's wrist looked like. An intentionally created scar to create an artwork of some sort, although I couldn't tell what from the small snippet that was offered. A tattoo wouldn't have surprised me, they were hardly taboo anymore, but scarification stunned me for a moment, and my gaze lingered longer than it should have. Long enough for Mike to notice and subtly pull down his sleeve and adjust the cufflink, although he didn't look at me after that for the remainder of the meeting, and I wondered if I'd discovered some secret part of him he didn't want anyone to know about.

The thought was enticing, and I *did* want to know more.

The meeting concluded with another round of handshakes, and since I needed to be getting back to work myself, I offered to walk Mike out of the building. He smiled at me before a snippet of a frown flashed on his face, followed by a hesitation in his movements. Was he *that* bothered I had seen the marks on his arm?

Stepping into the elevator alone with Mike sent the temperature up ninety degrees, or that's what it felt like.

"So…" Mike said, leaning against the side of the elevator, "… you want to follow in your father's footsteps?"

I smiled for a moment before it dropped, and I lifted a shoulder in a shrug. "To be honest, not really."

Mike smirked. "Yeah, I didn't think so. So what were you doing here today?"

I wanted to say something smooth like *I was waiting for you,* or *I wanted to see if you lived up to your reputation,* and while the thought of such cheesy pick-up lines made me grin, in my head was where they stayed. "Dad offered, and it seemed rude to turn him down."

Mike hummed. "So, in other words, you didn't

know how to politely say, 'Actually, Dad, I'd rather stay at home and watch football, or do literally anything else than come into your corporate world.'"

I laughed. "I'm more into baseball myself."

Mike chuckled as the elevator dinged, and an unnecessarily seductive electronic voice announced we were on the ground floor. We exited, close enough to be holding hands but avoiding touching each other while we at least tried to keep professional. I wondered if his thoughts were straying where mine were.

I couldn't wait. "Could I take you out to dinner?"

Mike stopped as we exited the building, looking down the street toward where his office building stood before he rested his gaze on mine. He was unreadable, and I waited for a smile that didn't come. The seconds stretched out, and he seemed to be fighting some internal battle, his eyes darting between mine. I dropped my gaze to his hand, double-checking for a wedding ring, and released a sigh when there was none. It was then there was a flicker of a smirk from Mike.

"No," he said finally, and I took a step back from him as the disappointment washed over me. "But *I* will take *you* out to dinner."

We stared at each other for a beat, and while I don't know what he was thinking, I was *definitely* thinking of peeling that shirt from his body and getting my hands on his chest, wondering what his weight would feel like on top of me. Releasing a long breath, I ran my hand through my thick, golden blond hair. "You got me," I finally said. It sounded lame, but I was too distracted to come up with much else.

The smile from Mike was genuine, but there was concern in his eyes. With a flick of his nimble fingers, he handed me a business card. "Text me your address, and I'll pick you up at seven." Mike's gaze wandered my body in the same way mine had his when he first walked into my father's office. "I assumed you meant tonight?"

I could barely find my breath, let alone my words, as the imagery of the things I wanted to do with this man came back in full force, pushing all other logical and sound thoughts from my head to the point I'm surprised I wasn't gaping at him like a fish out of water. Something flashed across his eyes, and I'm certain, at that moment, he knew exactly what I was thinking.

Why couldn't I control these thoughts? Mike simply radiated power. I pocketed the business card without looking at it.

"Yeah..." I said, swallowing heavily before smiling at him. "Tonight is fine."

CHAPTER 4

MIKE

What was it about Jacob that had made me accept his offer for dinner?

Although I'd taken the power back by making it clear *I* was taking *him* out and not the other way around, I could have left my answer at a simple *no,* and in hindsight, I should have. I was hardly celibate, but I'd also made a promise to myself not to get close enough to another human to even *consider* bonding again. Not after Tate.

I had loved Tate. I truly did. And perhaps a part of me always would. He was kind to me, in the beginning, at least, and one of the few humans who could make me feel safe. To feel as though he would take down anyone in his way who kept him from my side. There was a fire behind his eyes, a desire to please, but also a desire to gain power and to lead. That was our downfall.

Tate was only nineteen when we met, and it wasn't long before we bonded. I had been on Earth for only a handful of years and never considered that being with a human could feel the way it did with him. I realize now how inexperienced and foolish I was. I got swept up by him and the rush of emotions that flooded my chest, making my heart pound harder every time he was near.

I loved him, but I didn't know who he was.

A broken man taught how to survive by the worst of humankind, cast to the side and treated as second best, nothing Tate did was ever good enough for his father. I thought we were a comfort for each other, and when we were together, none of the other issues mattered. Foolishly, I thought I was enough for Tate.

But when we bonded and my blood flowed through his veins, he gained some of my strength and enhanced senses and power. Then everything that was dark about his humanity rose to the surface, and he changed. Were *all* those aspects of him present before we bonded? Possibly. But it was impossible for me to separate the act of our bonding with him becoming a darker version of himself. It was my fault he changed, and I shouldn't have let him get as close as he did.

I should never have let my blood touch his tongue.

He became violent afterward but never with me. I was many decades older and more powerful, and he was only a human with a few enhanced abilities, but he started testing the limits of his strength. When he attacked a young woman and told me of his plans to use his powers to kill whoever he needed to in order to take over his father's business, dread crept through me. Tate wanted me to be *happy* for him, for him embracing his own demon so thoroughly. But I wanted to escape that part of me, and the reminder of who I was inside stood in front of me every day, claiming he loved me back. But if Tate ever did love me, it was all pushed to the side when he realized the extent of his newfound powers. He was everything I hated about demons in the flesh. I hated the lust for violence, and worse than that, I hated the pleasure that was taken in it. Everything about who I was under this skin was torture to me, and I had enough reminders of my need to suppress it without the presence of Tate lying through his teeth about his feelings for me. Now, all that was moot.

I'd wanted to sever the bond.

Tate told me I wasn't a demon at all and was weak and pathetic.

And maybe he was right.

So now, I kept my distance from humans, emotionally. Frank came to Earth to join me a few years after I severed the bond with Tate, and to this day, I hadn't told him the full story. The scars left after the severing ran across my skin like deep rope burns that wound their way across my torso, arms, and legs, ending at my wrists and ankles. Any demon looking at me would know immediately what the scars meant, and thankfully, they all knew better than to ask.

I focused on building my business, and now we were expanding, I could move away from here.

Thankfully.

The demon population in this city was growing. Granted, it was mostly down south where crime was more prevalent, but I wanted out of here before this city became Hell on Earth, and moving to another state for my business and starting over sounded perfect.

San Francisco, I wanted to go to San Francisco.

Then I had strolled into that damn office and saw Jacob, and all that had been pushed from my mind as effectively as sweeping my arm across my desk and knocking everything to the floor.

Which, if his father hadn't been there, is exactly what I would have done and taken Jacob on the desk right there. The way his eyes blazed when he saw me told me he would have not only let me do it, but would have thrown himself at me with equal vigor. He had a casual stance, leaning against the desk with his arms folded over his chest, not as built or as tall as Frank or me but could hold his own.

Something about him looked out of place in his white office shirt tucked so neatly into his gray pants. His shoes were too scuffed, like he worked somewhere he could get dirty, and the uneven tan lines around his wrists and neck told me he was outside as much as he was in.

Yeah, I got a good look at him.

I wondered what he did in his free time, but I wasn't there to ask about his life. I was there for business, always for business, which I reminded myself of constantly during the meeting when his eyes kept meeting mine. We both knew neither of us was concentrating on the plans and designs on the desk between us.

Pure fucking chemistry.

Frank would tell me to go for it, to take Jacob out and fuck him senseless.

But would I corrupt him the same way I had Tate?

Surely, I could have one night with him, and he would be safe from me.

Just one night.

Another suit, evening wear, black on black.

I slid into the driver's seat of my car after getting out to open the door for Jacob. He eyed me with a smirk, somewhere between suspicion and amusement, as I did and chuckled lightly when I lightly slapped his hand out of the way and buckled his seat belt for him. Despite all the parts of myself I denied, demons were not submissive, and even if this were only for one night, I needed it to be abundantly clear who was in charge.

Jacob didn't seem to mind.

The restaurant was expensive, several blocks from the proposed site of the new apartment building I had discussed with Jacob's father only hours before. Neither of us mentioned it. Jacob had already professed his disinterest in his father's work, and I was far from focused on that tonight. The idea of being close to him had stirred something in me and offered a reminder as to why I don't indulge in this side more often. Even the smallest hint of sex had my demon riling up, preparing to take over, to let loose and dominate. And Jacob smelled amazing beyond the subtle, spicy cologne covering the scent of his skin. If I concentrated, I could almost hear his blood pulsing through his veins. His heart was pumping faster than normal, and I'm certain it's because his mind was in the same place as mine.

Back at my place, on the bed, sweaty and naked, him at my mercy.

I wondered if I still had those silk ties around because I could picture Jacob's lithe figure on the bed underneath me, the ties straining as he pulled against them, gyrating and grinding against the air, desperate for friction.

Fuck.

Concentrate.

One did not gain control of their demon for over a decade by letting it take back that control every time sex was on the mind.

The valet caught my car keys as I tossed them underhand over my car, and he slid sleekly into my front seat as if he owned the vehicle. Little was said, they were too professional for that, and I preferred it that way. Placing my palm on the small of Jacob's back, he smirked again in that bemused way but didn't stop me, only speaking once we were seated and the waiter had disappeared after taking my wine order.

"You like to be in control, don't you?" Jacob asked. The question was paired with a sweep of his hand through his hair, a motion that appeared casual, but coupled with the darting of his eyes around the room, it displayed his nervousness. He wasn't used to places like this, and internally I cursed myself for picking such a high-end restaurant. Jacob was more casual, and I'm certain he would have been happy if we'd gotten drive-through burgers and sat in the car in the parking lot, laughing between bites.

My lips lifted into a smirk of my own. *Did I like being in control?* "You have no idea," I rumbled, holding his eye contact long enough for Jacob to be certain there was something to be heard between the lines.

His chuckle ended, and he licked his lips, opening his mouth to reply and stopping when the waiter returned and poured our drinks, leaving the bottle on the table as indicated.

"Aren't you going to take a taste and say..." Jacob smacked his lips obscenely, drawing a glance from the couple at the table next to us and making me grin, "... *hmm , yes, rather good. This will do, I suppose, Jeeves.*"

"Nice of you to learn the waiter's name so quickly."

"You're *kidding.*"

Chuckling, I nodded. "Of course I am."

Jacob laughed. "Payback for me mocking you, I suppose."

My smile was dangerous. "Absolutely." There was a moment of silence as we both took a drink, perusing the menu. "So tell me, Jacob, if you don't want to work for the council or the mayor, what do you want to do?"

"I'm an accountant."

"That's not what I asked."

His eyes narrowed, and his lips lifted into a smirk

again. It seemed his default expression, as though inside his head were his own personal jokes he thought no one else would find funny, so he kept them to himself. "I'm uh…" he took another drink, steeling himself up to tell me something shocking perhaps, "… a mechanic."

Not what I expected. "By trade?"

"Not yet. I was taught by a friend."

"Sometimes that's the best way."

"Agreed. While his memory wasn't as good as it was when he was younger, even the things he'd forgotten probably covered more than modern mechanics ever learned. I want to work on classic cars mainly, and I would *love* to have my own business." He paused as though once he started talking about it, it all came tumbling out, and he caught himself too late. Absentmindedly, he ran his fingers delicately over the stem of the wine glass, and I studied his hands. I can't believe I hadn't noticed it before, the slight callousing, the remnants of dirt and oil under his nails that would never go away no matter how much he cleaned them. Maybe he didn't want to clean it, maybe it was a reminder to himself of what he was truly passionate about. Maybe it was a subtle, perhaps even subconscious, fuck you to what was expected of him.

"So what's stopping you?" I asked.

Jacob eyed me again, another sweep of his hand through his hair, his fingers combing back the blond locks. A motion I hoped to do myself later. "It's not that simple."

"It rarely is. I wasn't claiming it was. I asked, what's stopping you?"

"Usually, when people say that, they mean *why haven't you just done it already?*"

"Maybe, but that's not what I meant."

"There are expectations, you know? Dad is so keen for me to follow him career-wise, but there is a world of things I'd rather do between mechanic, the dream, and city planner, the last resort. Did you see my graduation photo on his desk today?" I nodded, and Jacob dipped his chin before continuing. "He's so proud of me, and he's never been anything but supportive, but the longer I leave it, the harder it gets to raise the topic, and whenever I mention work, he immediately begins talking about his, as though they're one-in-the-same—his work and mine." Jacob took another sip of his wine, again licking his lips and again making me think things about his lips and mouth I shouldn't be in a crowded restaurant. "But enough about me, tell me your story."

"I'm an architect."

He laughed, and I smirked. "No shit. Tell me all the usual first-date stuff. How did you get into it? Why do you love it? Do you have any siblings, etcetera, etcetera?"

"How did we get from business to siblings?"

Jacob lifted a shoulder, his eyes flashing with a cheekiness that he displayed on the forefront of his personality. "As I said, general first-date questions."

"I got into architecture because I enjoy creating and making something out of nothing. I chose architecture instead of art because I have a big ego, and I'm a control freak, and creating buildings is far grander than painting on a canvas or building a birdhouse."

"Big ego and a control freak? Starting off with honesty."

"You already know I like to be in control."

Jacob chuckled, and we held eye contact. Again, for longer than was necessary and communicating all things that neither of us were going to voice just yet. "And the siblings?" he asked.

"I have many brothers and sisters, none of which I see."

"Why?"

"We don't get along."

That slight smirk was coupled with unasked questions in his eyes, but it seemed he didn't want to get into that line of questioning any more than I did, and the conversation moved forward. The waiter returned shortly to take our orders, and Jacob joked about me ordering for him, which I proceeded to do.

He really did need to learn who was in control here.

CHAPTER
5

JACOB

Dinner was pleasant, more than pleasant. Mike was a gentleman in every way, although occasionally, we would share a look, and his eyes would blaze with intensity as he stared me down, a challenge that wasn't verbalized but which I already knew I was going to take him up on.

Do you think you could handle me?

Fuck, he was hot, and getting sexier with every minute that passed. Every word from his mouth was gold, nothing seemed rehearsed or stoic, yet he continued to hold that graceful, professional demeanor about him, as though he was in complete control all the time. And with the ballet of the staff around him, I guess he did. He owned the situation, knew what would happen before it did, commanded attention without having to raise his voice, and held a conversation that was the perfect combination of flirting and actual getting-to-know-you style questions.

I was somehow relaxed in an atmosphere that would generally put me on edge.

So when he invited me back to his place for a drink, I didn't hesitate.

I didn't fight him this time as he held the car door open for me and latched my seat belt. I liked the brush of his hands over my body as he drew the seat belt across my chest and the touch of his fingers on my outer thigh as the buckle clicked into place. Mike's eyes met mine, and again, there was that moment that lasted just a touch longer than expected of two casual acquaintances, a look that promised so much without saying anything.

The urge to kiss him then and there was strong, but I held back. As he drove, I rested my hand on his thigh, a touch that made him start slightly and swallow nervously, the first hint I had seen that he wasn't in as much control as he portrayed.

I liked that side of him, and part of me wanted to make him lose control, to see what animal lay beneath the suit.

Mike's penthouse apartment was almost as intimidating as the restaurant—picture-perfect like it was straight out of a catalog, every piece of furniture in its place, all perfectly color and style coordinated, exactly as you would expect for someone of his wealth. But there was something off about it. There wasn't a personal memento in sight, not a framed photograph or an out-of-place knickknack, such as when someone gifts you something, and although it doesn't match your existing décor, you display it anyway because you love it and the person it came from. But there was nothing.

"Nice place," I said, shrugging off my jacket and looking for a place to hang it as we crossed the threshold. Mike ushered me in gently with a warm hand on the small of my back. He took the jacket from me, laid it carefully over the back of one of the dining room chairs, and moved away to make drinks.

Mike smirked. "Thank you, but I can't tell if you're being sarcastic or not."

"Not exactly, I don't think. I guess it just doesn't feel like there's anything of you in this place, nothing personal."

Mike's movement paused in his ministrations of mixing bourbon-based cocktails, and he seemed to be rolling my statement around in his mind, trying to figure out the correct response. Had he had it pointed out to him before? Surely, he'd had other men in his apartment, and it wasn't exactly hard to notice.

"I don't like to get attached," he said finally.

It was a hint and a warning that wasn't lost on

me. He might as well have said that tonight was a one-night stand and nothing more. If I were being honest with myself, I would have admitted this disappointed me—there seemed so much more to Mike than what was on the surface. But the chemistry between us was electric, and if that's what I needed to agree to for a chance to get my hands on him, then I would do what he was comfortable with.

Approaching the small corner bar, I leaned my forearms on the counter as Mike slid my drink to me, the sound of the glass on marble cutting through the silence and the anticipation. We sipped our drinks in silence for a few moments, not breaking eye contact, each daring the other to make the first move while equally enjoying the self-inflicted torture of the tease.

Visions of getting Mike naked flashed across my mind, and it became impossible to push the thoughts away. A particularly strong image of Mike looming over me while he penetrated me had my breath hitching, and I coughed slightly on my drink. Mike's eyebrows shot up, and his grin suggested he knew exactly what I'd been thinking. Coming around from behind the bar, Mike dragged his glass along the counter as he approached, and when he was chest to chest with me, I stared up at him, begging my body not to betray my need and start trembling before he had even touched me.

My lips parted slightly, but I had no idea what I planned on saying.

Mike merely watched me, and I got the sense he enjoyed the game.

"Isn't this a conflict of interest?" I whispered, half joking and entirely not caring if it was.

"I don't give a fuck about work right now. I have other things on my mind."

"Like what?"

Oh God, I wanted to hear this man talk dirty to me.

A low growl rumbled through Mike's throat, and he took a half step forward, forcing me to move back. His hand swept around my lower back again, holding me against him so every breath caused my chest to brush against his. "Like how you'd look tied to my bed, naked and begging for my cock."

Fuck.

There weren't any words, and even if there were, I don't think I could form a complete sentence right now. My mind was a mess from his proximity, scent, and body's heat against mine. The bedroom seemed too far away, and I wanted to pull him to the floor now, but Mike's grip on the back of my shirt made it clear he was in charge. He was going to lead this night, to take control and give the orders, and I was there only to give and receive pleasure.

Yes, please.

"Mike..." I whispered. He had lowered his face close to mine, and the words were a brush of air against his lips. When he kissed me, it was slow, hesitant, and decadent. He was taking his time tasting and touching, his little finger brushing my back where he held my shirt, now slightly bunched under his hand and lifting from my pants. A few more inches and his hand would be on my bare skin, and I wiggled slightly, trying to speed up the process. Mike chuckled against my lips, increasing the desperation of the kiss, using his tongue to claim, and sending my heartbeat skyrocketing. When he ran his fingers through my hair, a growl moved through his chest again, and I groaned against his lips.

"You want to be used, don't you?" Mike crooned, and when I moved to nod, his grip on my hair tightened, holding my head still. "Good."

With only the slightest pressure, he encouraged me to drop to my knees, and my hands were on his belt buckle before I had even reached the floor. The marble was cool, and felt good on my skin even through my pants, and the metal of his belt buckle warmed up quickly under my eager fingers. Mike brushed his hands through my hair, touching his thumbs against my cheeks and lips as I undid his fly. When I went to pull his pants down, his grip on my head increased, and he barked, "No. Leave them on."

Whatever. I got it. Some guys liked to remain fully dressed—it wasn't something I hadn't encountered before. From my experience, remaining clothed was a power thing, especially while your partner is naked. So, I loosened his pants just enough to pull his waiting cock free, already hard and ready for me, the tip dripping with precum. Mike closed his eyes and tilted his head back as I licked from the base to the tip, taking my time the same way he had with the kiss, and he let me.

For a while.

Soon, his grip on my hair got tighter, and when I teased him again with another lick, flicking my tongue over the head, he growled, thrust forward, and shoved his length into my mouth.

Use me.

And he did, holding my head while he fucked my mouth, grunts and groans emanating from his lips. Mike was rushing toward his climax, using me to get off, chasing the high. I felt I should be offended by this behavior, by being pushed to my knees and forced to swallow around his hard cock, but it was fucking *hot,* and I wanted *more.*

Moaning around his length as he sped up again, I gripped his thighs with both hands, steadying myself against the onslaught of his thrusts. I could feel he was close by the way he hardened that little bit more in my mouth and the change of tone of his moans, now closer to animalistic growls. I wanted to know if he'd make those same sounds when he fucked me, and the thought made me harder than I already was as Mike groaned, gripped my head and held me in place while he came in my mouth. The salty tang splashed down my throat, and I struggled to swallow while his cock remained hard between my lips, pumping in and out slowly while Mike came down from his high. His eyes were closed again, and he sighed as he pulled from my mouth.

Bending, Mike grabbed me under my elbows and helped me to my feet before running his thumb along my bottom lip. "Sorry," he muttered. "I just had to fuck that perfect mouth."

His words and the heavy erotic quality of his voice sent another shock wave of heat through my body, and I responded by running my palms down his chest, coming to rest on his cock, still hard and ready to go again.

"Fuck me, please." My words were almost lost as he pressed his lips to mine, dancing his tongue across mine and tasting himself on me. I loved how a growl rumbled through his chest whenever he touched me and his hands tightened on me, claiming me.

He chuckled, tracing his fingers down my jawline until his hand was around my neck, and he held my eye contact as he tightened his grip slightly, only enough to remind me who was in charge. His eyes were searching mine, perhaps looking for hesitation, but all he would find would be lust and desire, and I squeezed him in response, making him grunt.

"You love it, don't you?" he whispered, his breath warm against my neck as he nipped lightly at my skin. "Being used by me? You'd love for me to bend you over right here and take you."

"God, yes. Please…"

I started unbuttoning his shirt and got to the fourth one before he pulled from me, his hands grabbing mine with a speed and strength that startled me. "No…" he whispered, gently returning my hands to my sides, "… leave my clothes on."

"But I want to touch you."

"You can touch me over my shirt."

It wasn't the same, and I couldn't help the slight frown that dimpled my forehead as I watched him. Was he hiding something? "Does this have anything to do with your scarification?"

"My what?"

Reaching up, I touched his wrist where I had seen the marks on his skin earlier. "The artwork on your wrists. Does it cover your chest too? Do you not want me to see it?"

Mike's back stiffened, and the air grew cold between us. The step he took away from me might have well been a mile, and the significance of the gesture was greater than the space he had created. Barely two inches, but it felt like more.

"It's not artwork," he finally grumbled out.

"What is it?"

I knew I shouldn't push, as though his body language wasn't already clear enough, but there was something dangerous in his eyes—a darkness bordered by regret. I could understand if he was young when he got the scarification done and regretted it now, but he didn't need to hide himself from me. I wouldn't judge. I only wanted to touch him, to feel him closer to me.

I told him as much, and he turned his head from me.

Another step back, and the distance increased.

Less than five minutes ago, he was fucking my mouth as though he owned me, and now he was looking anywhere but at me. I was no stranger to rejection, but this was cutting on an entirely different level.

"What are the scars?" When he didn't answer, I repeated my earlier sentiment. "You don't have to hide from me... I'm not going to judge you. I only want to touch you."

When I stepped toward Mike, he stepped back again.

His position was clear.

"They're from the last person I let get close to me."

What the fuck?

Did someone fucking *attack* him? A psycho ex? It

was hard to imagine Mike in a situation where he wasn't the alpha, the dominant of the other, but his demeanor had changed. However slight, there was a nervousness to his movements now. While his posture remained perfect and his expression almost impassive, the slightest frown formed along with the subtle drumming of his fingers on the marble bar.

"I... I'm sorry." I didn't know what to say. I pulled forward in my memory the image I had captured of the scars on his wrist. What could have created something like that? A rope burn? Being restrained? A hot poker? None of the options reduced the sick feeling in my stomach.

"I think you should go," Mike said, the finality of his tone not backed up by the uncertainty on his face.

"I can stay," I offered. I didn't want to leave him, not now, not like this.

"No."

"Can I see you for dinner again?"

"I don't think that's a good idea."

My patience came to an abrupt end. "What the fuck, Mike? It's not like I'm asking you to marry me."

Mike simply shook his head, backing away from me as though I was poison.

"You don't understand," Mike muttered. The pain in his tone tugged at something in my chest, but it was difficult now not to feel completely used and not in a fucking good way. I wanted to feel used, lying in bed beside him, naked and exhausted. Not used, my jaw slightly sore from his rough fucking, with a man who now refused to look at me. He reached forward as though he was going to take my hand, then thought the better of it and dropped his arm back to his side. "Even this close..." Mike waved his hand dismissively in the space between us, indicating where we had been standing together, "... is too close."

"So why ask me to dinner? Why..." I couldn't even bring myself to say *fuck my mouth*, but I didn't need to as Mike's gray eyes dropped back to the floor. He had no answers for me, and I wasn't going to get anything more from him. All the sophisticated persona, it was all bullshit. Everything was grandstanding, a normal person afraid of any sort of commitment, even though I had made no mention or attempted to get anything more from him than something casual. It would be nice, but I wasn't going to push. It was one date, for fuck's sake.

Underneath it all, Mike was nothing but a...

"Coward," I whispered.

Mike's eyes shot up and met mine, and for a moment, there was a flare of possessiveness again before the guilt came back, and he looked away from me—this time across his apartment and out the window at the dark cityscape outside.

"Fuck this." Striding away from Mike, I grabbed my jacket on the way out and didn't look back.

CHAPTER
6

MIKE

Coward.

Jacob wasn't wrong.

I was a coward.

I was a coward when it came to Tate and how I handled the situation—any other demon wouldn't have had a problem with his violent tendencies, and if they did, they would have taken him down and be damned with the consequences.

Any other demon wouldn't have bonded so frivolously.

And I was a coward when it came to moving on.

It had been almost a decade, and I remained hiding behind my suits, figuratively and literally. On the rare occasions I fucked, I fucked with my clothes on, and most of the men didn't complain. They were never denied pleasure, so why shouldn't they let me have what they assumed was a kink of mine?

Except Jacob.

Of course, he would be the type to question me, with understanding and lust in his eyes, wanting to touch and be close, wanting to feel his hands on my chest, then over my shoulders and into my hair as I returned the favor he had done for me, and shown him what magic I could do with *my* mouth. But because there was something about him that drew me to him—a passion and electricity that made him different—that was all the more reason not to let him get closer than he already had.

It was a mistake to go on a date, and it was a mistake to bring him back to my place.

But I was finding it hard to regret the feeling of his lips wrapped around my cock.

There was one thing I wanted to ask the werewolves to do before I stopped seeing the pack, and it's something I should have asked of them a long time ago.

But Jacob was right.

Coward.

Now I was fueled with self-hatred, and my hands were balled into fists at my sides as I strode through the wet grass, knee-high and leaving my pants soaked. Jacob deserved much better than the likes of me, and while I enjoyed living a life of luxury I had built here, that's all I should be aiming for.

I was no good for humans.

Tate had proven that to me.

"Fuck," I cursed out loud, letting the word push through my gritted teeth and increasing my stride until I was just short of running. "Dante!"

I knew he could hear me. He would have heard me approaching half a mile back and would be sitting and waiting, unable to get my scent as I was downwind. But now he would know it was me, and he could come and meet me halfway. More than halfway, he could cross more ground on four legs than I could on two.

The gray wolf approached, and I didn't flinch or slow in my stride. He came straight at me, moving majestically through the grass, crashing through the undergrowth where the edge of the field met the woods, hours outside of the city. If he wanted to, he could move with such stealth that even a demon would have difficulty knowing he was coming, but this wasn't about stealth. Dante had already told me I wasn't welcome, and I was risking my life by being here and his if he were to be seen as sympathetic toward me.

Front paws collided with my chest, knocking me off my feet, and as we fell together, Dante transformed back into human, naked and pinning me down, his long fingernails digging into my shoulders. My forward momentum had done nothing to save myself from being knocked over, and Dante bared his teeth at me, growling and snarling, his face making the last shift back into human as the gray fur disappeared.

"What the fuck are you doing here?" he roared.

"I have a favor to ask."

Dante snarled again. "Our truce was temporary, and I trusted you to stay away when I asked. You've betrayed that trust. I should kill you."

"No." His eyebrows flickered at my response before settling back into a deep frown. "Not death, that's not what I ask of you. I want you to destroy my mark."

His grip on my shoulders eased only slightly. "Why?"

"I should have done it years ago when I first found you. I'll never be going back to Hell, so I don't need it. If I can't live on Earth, I'd rather be dead."

Dante's gaze shifted to my chest, where concealed beneath my windbreaker my mark lay, hidden until I drew on my demonic powers to bring it to the surface. The mark of the pentagram etched into demons' skin allowed us to move between worlds—Hell and Earth. When a demon was banished from Hell, the mark would be destroyed, torn from the body, and the demon would not be able to return to Hell. If you died once your mark had been destroyed, you remained dead.

"It's a painful process."

"I know," I said, holding his eye contact. Dante and the others would have to literally tear the skin from me, creating five cuts, and in their wolf forms, shred the pentagram apart.

More scars to add to my collection.

I no longer cared.

We stared at each other for a long time. Meanwhile, three other wolves approached, the remainder of the pack—one black, one white, and one reddish brown. They were the only ones near enough to this city to meet even semi-regularly before they returned to their solitary lives and territories. I couldn't see them through the darkness, but I heard them approach, could smell the dampness of their fur, and if they shifted their silhouette, were barely visible in my peripheral vision. But I dared not tear my gaze from Dante. He was the main threat right now, and whatever past we had meant nothing, based on a flimsy understanding and respect, which I had destroyed the remainder of when I came here against his wishes.

"I don't know if I can do that for you," Dante finally said.

"Why not?"

"Because it's a favor, as you said. We cannot be seen as friends. I took a risk allowing you to be around us in the first place, but that has to end. If I don't fulfill my duty..." He trailed off, but I already knew.

As a human who traded his destined place in Hell

for a life as a werewolf, the deal would be broken if he didn't take care of demons and transitional souls as he was meant to. A lifetime on Earth as a werewolf was nothing compared to an eternity in Hell, and he had opted to give up this life to save his soul.

I was a risk to him.

I tilted my head toward the nearest wolf. I couldn't see who it was, but I suspected it was Bane. "I'm sure your friends would appreciate the opportunity to tear apart a demon."

His words were minced with another snarl. "We don't do this for *fun!*" he roared at me.

Making him angry would not help my cause, but I felt this was my last chance, and I wouldn't be able to get this close again. If I tried to come back, they would take me down before I even came to the edge of the wooded area.

Dropping my tone, I grabbed his wrists. "Dante, please."

His eyes changed, turning yellow for a moment. The irony wasn't lost on me. A demon in natural form had yellow eyes, and it was usually the first thing to change when we lost control. But instead of black slits for pupils, Dante's were round like that of his wolf form.

He sighed heavily and looked to his side. Bane had approached, the large black wolf close enough now to latch his jaws around my neck. Bane's head inclined, barely a noticeable movement. Still on top of me, Dante gained my eye contact again. "Would you like to be unconscious? To avoid the worst of the pain."

I shouldn't.

I deserved the pain.

I should take the punishment to remind me how weak I really was, that I wasn't a true demon, denying my instincts as I did. I wasn't human. I was instead a monster living amongst them, punishment I deserved for corrupting Tate and hurting Jacob.

Punishment for the fact I wanted to get closer to Jacob when I should have known better.

But I was a coward.

"Yes," I whispered, unable to look Dante in the eye.

"Very well."

Coward.

I heard movement near me, and then everything went black.

When the cravings started, they built up in my stomach, almost indistinguishable from hunger

for a few minutes at least. But then they grew from a simple craving, as though for a sweet after a nice meal, into desire and then into need. A need that pulses through the blood, reaching the heart and head and forcing its way outward. A desire that makes itself known, telling you in no uncertain terms that if the desire is not met, then we have no choice, and our demon forms will take over and take what we need.

Because in Hell, there's no denying these desires. In Hell, sex and violence abound, and we simply take what we want because all the others want it too.

On Earth, violence is frowned upon, and human blood can send demons into a frenzy. A controlled fight with a human is something that can only be achieved with time and practice at keeping control. Demon blood doesn't smell as sweet and doesn't make us want to taste it. And if a demon kills a human, then we're taken by the werewolves, the hellhounds, and never allowed to return to Earth.

But I was denying my cravings and desires, and I had been since I stepped foot on this plane. Determined not to give in, the hunger had grown until my muscles rippled underneath my clothes, threatening to tear apart and unleash the monster that lived inside.

It was through sheer desperation that I let go,

just a little bit, just enough to get it back under control. But I was too rough with him, the man I picked up at the bar. I didn't hurt him, thankfully, but I scared him. The need to dominate ran thick through my blood. He wanted lovemaking, but instead, I fucked him ruthlessly, fast, and hard until he was coming with me, the words 'slow down' on the edge of his tongue as his cum spilled on the bedsheets.

I'd been on Earth for only a matter of months and was coming to accept that I couldn't keep myself under control through willpower alone. I don't think any demon could. That's why they fought, fucked, ran amok, and did as they pleased. Mostly.

So I needed an outlet, and that was when I found the weres.

It was an accident. I certainly wasn't looking for the very creatures who were designed to take me down if I stepped out of line. But the animalistic therapy *poster in the local café sparked my interest. What was the premise? You and several other people hang out in a field in the middle of the night and scream at the moon. Sounds ridiculous? I thought so too. But at that point, I was willing to try anything to keep my demon down and not have to fight my way free of the urges, and I was running out of options. Some cathartic screaming might do the trick.*

Maybe.

So I had showed up to the first meeting and recognized the scent of werewolves immediately. Not everyone in the group, that would be too many for the area, but two of them definitely—Bane and Dante—and they recognized me at the same moment I did them.

Howling at the moon for therapy to get back in touch with your wild roots *made complete sense that the group would be hosted by werewolves. It would be the only time they could have company, and their wolfish behavior wouldn't get them caught out, where they could feel at one with the wolf that resided inside them and continue to keep human company without having to stamp down their true nature.*

I was familiar with that feeling.

But they didn't want me there. The humans had dispersed after the meeting, patting each other on the back and feeling free. They'd start laughing at the ridiculousness of the situation once shame crept back into their minds the further they moved from the emptiness of the field. After everyone else had left, that's when Dante and Bane came for me. I didn't run since weres can outrun demons, and I found myself pinned in the grass, teeth near my face and jaws snapping at my neck as they changed into wolf form mid-takedown.

I should have fought for my life, but werewolves

were stronger than demons, and the pathetic part of it was I no longer wanted to fight. For some inconceivable reason, the cathartic screaming had somewhat helped, and I was certain if the weres would give me the time, together we could figure out a solution that would allow me to control my urges and remain on Earth. As soon as I felt their presence, I had also felt a jump of hope. Not because I wanted them to put me out of my misery but because werewolves offered the control I desired. They could guide and keep me protected if needed.

But they had a job to do and had traded their souls as humans under the promise they would do it.

So when they started to tear me apart, I didn't fight them off.

Demons healed fast, but not fast enough to keep our skin together when two werewolves were so hell-bent on tearing it apart. My chest was in shreds, and my heart one good bite away from being torn from my body when they stopped. One of the wolves shifted back into human form with the cracking of bones and whimpers from the pain before he looked at me, his shaggy hair falling in front of his face and haunted eyes.

"Why don't you fight back, demon?" he demanded of me.

I had to cough up a good volume of blood before

I could get the words out, gargling in my throat as my body fought to heal itself in the precious seconds before I would be attacked again. "I don't want to be a demon."

"Do you want to die?"

"No, but if I can't control my urges without violence, I would rather be dead."

The other were had shifted too, and the two men glanced at each other over my bloody body, sharing something significant between them. Both men radiated the aura of alpha males, perhaps not as arrogant as demons, but there was no way these two lived together. If they did, they'd tear each other apart over the smallest disagreement. Werewolves generally didn't do well in the company of others of their kind for too long.

The second man spoke. Previously in his wolf form, he was large and covered in black fur, and the beard that covered most of his face was the same shiny black and covered anything that would resemble an expression while his dark eyes spoke worlds.

"If you make it through the night, demon..." he drawled, pushing himself to his feet, "... then we will talk next time we meet."

They left, and through an act of submission and honesty about my desire to be rid of my demonic urges, they had spared my life.

The wounds would be slow to heal.

It was four hours before I could drag myself back to my car, and my extremities were numb from the night air while my circulation system focused on returning blood to my healing chest. It was another two hours before I could drive home, and after that, I spent three days in bed.

But I made it, and I would need to return to see the wolves again.

Hours later, I awoke, and the dreams which were memories of the first time I had met Dante and Bane swirled in my head. The werewolves were gone when I regained consciousness, and their last act of mercy had been to bandage my chest where they had destroyed my mark. I didn't bother to peel back the gauze to see the damage. I trusted them to have done what they needed to do, and judging by the way my skin felt like it was going to split open as I stood, it certainly seemed as though the pentagram had been removed correctly.

That was it. There would be no returning to Hell for me. If I died on Earth, I died for good.

For over a decade, I had seen the werewolves at least once a month. Aside from the howling and screaming, which after time lost its ability to control my desires, Dante had come up with another idea. They allowed me to lose control, to turn into my full demon form, and I would wander the woods for hours while they guarded the perimeter and made sure I didn't leave the area.

They were there to take me down if I got out of control.

It worked, allowed me to stay in my true form safely for a period, which gave me the strength to keep balanced while I was in human form.

But that was over now, and I no longer had their protection or help. I couldn't blame them. They had taken a risk to help me at all, and I appreciated the time they had, but we weren't friends. That much was always clear.

Now I was on my own, and until I found another means of control, I was even more dangerous to be around.

Which meant I couldn't risk allowing myself to be anywhere near Jacob, let alone entertain the idea of dating.

Does personal sacrifice make me any less of a coward?

Probably not.

CHAPTER
7

JACOB

This was getting out of hand, and I couldn't let it drag on much longer.

Dad had mistook my keen attitude in the meeting the other day with Mike as my growing interest in the business, and how could I tell him otherwise? Especially after the way my date with Mike had turned out—an absolute train wreck of a night. Which was beyond a pity because he was an absolute gentleman and had all the right levels of domination once we were alone. I still hadn't figured out what I'd done so wrong that Mike needed to turn me away as harshly as he did, but at least he had the sense to look ashamed of his behavior. It was difficult because I was certain there was some deep trauma and pain behind his actions, and the implication his scars were caused by an ex was more than I could take.

So while I sat in my cubicle, working on yet another spreadsheet to show a client for the fourth time if he continued his same spending patterns, then he was going to be bankrupt within two years, my thoughts wandered. Because I was still drawn to Mike, perhaps even more than before. When I met him, he was a dashing man in an expensive suit, someone who could show me a good time and be good company, but now there was more, and I wanted to know what his pain was.

I wanted to protect *him*.

However, he hardly seemed the type to let himself be protected.

My phone buzzed in my desk drawer, and while we weren't supposed to use our personal cell phones during office hours, I suspected no one would care much if I checked a text message. I had to resist the urge to groan and slump back into my chair because the message revealed Dad had made an executive decision that I was to hand deliver the second draft of the proposal back to Mike. Dad and his people had been over it, and the plans would go back and forth between them and the architecture firm several times, perhaps over months, until the final design and detailed specifications were settled.

Sounded like a riot.

Dad liked to work with paper rather than email,

and Mike humored him by printing out the designs on large rolls of paper and delivered them rather than sending an electronic copy.

The lie I'd built around myself simply couldn't continue, and soon I would have to come clean with my father about what I wanted to do. The problem was I wanted a plan *before* I had that conversation. I wanted to be able to go to him and say, *Dad, I want to be a mechanic. I've found a shop I can rent. I've saved this amount of money, and I have a business plan.*

Because I'd spent too much time already in denial about how much I truly hated my job, and while my business and accounting experience would come in handy when it came to running my own shop, I couldn't see myself chained to a desk for the rest of my life. Neither here nor working with Dad.

I could've told him no, and flicked back a text telling him I was too busy and couldn't get away to do the delivery.

But I wanted to see Mike for two reasons.

I wanted him to look me in the eye after how he had flipped out the other night, and perhaps it would draw from him not an apology but an explanation. Perhaps, like me, he would want to try a date again. Another date, another dinner, something more casual. Maybe I could take him out in my car, show him *my* passion because I certainly didn't want him to think I wanted a sugar daddy.

Secondly, because I wanted to be sure this chemistry I felt—the draw to this man—was more than simply my memories of him and my libido playing up and making it seem more than it actually was. Like when you share a flirty moment with a stranger in a bar, and you build it up in your mind the next day until you're convinced you had some sort of fairy-tale moment and you were long-lost soulmates from another life.

When really it was only flirting.

Apparently, absence makes the heart grow stupid as well as fonder.

And my heart liked to imagine all the wonderful scenarios with every attractive stranger I came across. But Mike wasn't a stranger, not anymore, not with the way he looked at me, and I couldn't tear my eyes from him. Not with the way he had touched me and taken control of my mouth and mind, and how he had laughed quietly, brushing his fingers along mine during dinner with a fleeting touch that promised pleasure.

Until that dark look crossed his eyes, and I knew he was capable of the best sort of power.

Making up some bogus excuse about having a medical appointment, I left the office for the day, heading straight to my father's office. I'd discarded my tie and untucked my shirt from my pants before I even arrived at his office, and Dad's expression was a mixture of amusement and exasperation. Smirking at him, I tucked my shirt back in, holding my arms out as if to ask *is that good enough?* Dad handed me the cardboard roll containing the latest plans and sent me on my way.

I knew he had mistaken my agreement as interest in the work, but I had been psyching myself up on the way over, getting ready to see Mike. Because I wanted to stand tall and stand my ground, and I wanted him to feel uncomfortable with what he had done. I had no reason to be embarrassed, so why should I? But it was difficult because whenever I would picture him staring down at me with those gray eyes, my mind would turn into a blank fog, and all I could think about was peeling his shirt back and finally getting my lips and tongue on his skin.

Stepping into the elevator to take me to Mike's office, I was somewhat curious to meet the infamous Frank and wondered if I'd have a chance to come across him. Mike tended to look after the repeat customers, the high-enders, while Frank focused on expanding the business, apparently able to talk his way into anyone's plans.

It took me a moment too long to realize when the elevator stopped on level three, the figure entering paused before coming to stand next to me, and the scent of him flared up the already scandalous thoughts I was having.

Mike stared at me. His eyes flickered from the

roll I held back to my face as I returned the look. I desperately wanted to break the silence that permeated the air between us, but I wanted him to break first because something told me he wasn't often the one to do precisely that.

But his gray eyes simply studied me, and I started drumming my fingers against the cardboard roll, the slight tapping sound the only thing other than the smooth mechanical whir of the elevator as it ascended.

I broke first.

"Hi," I said.

"Dropping off my plans, I see." Mike again eyed the roll in my hand and held his out to take it. "I'll take it now if you like."

"Don't you want to *bend me over right here and take me?*"

Mike's eyes widened, and his hand dropped back to his side. I resisted the urge to slap a hand over my mouth, having thrown his words back at him from the other night. Mike looked around the elevator car to check just in case someone had materialized since he stepped in and we were alone before he looked back at me. I wasn't usually quite so bold, although sometimes I wish I were, then perhaps I could have had the talk with my father about my career years ago. But there was something about Mike that called me to challenge him. I'd had a peek at the vulnerability underneath his suave demeanor, and I wanted to pick at it until he opened up to me again.

Maybe he was used to people dropping at his feet and doing as they were told, and while I'd be more than happy to partake in that level of submission with him in the bedroom, right here and now, I decided he needed someone like me to call him out on his shit.

Because you couldn't be sweet and kind and so fucking perfect on a date and then treat someone like shit because of some past thing you hadn't yet dealt with.

The elevator car felt like it was shrinking around us as he continued to stare at me, his expression hardened and his eyes boring into mine. The space around me closed in even more when Mike took one large stride forward, forcing me to back up against the wall. The cardboard roll hit the floor with a muffled thunk when Mike stretched his arm out, slapping the emergency stop on the elevator and bringing it to an abrupt halt between floors.

"Are you here just to be disrespectful, or do you have something to say?" Mike's voice rumbled out in what was almost a growl, and he boxed me into the space with his arms, placing a palm on either side of my head and leaning in until we were almost face to face.

"You were the one who was disrespectful, remember? Dad asked me to drop off the plans, and

I agreed."

"You really need to talk to him about your career plans," Mike said.

I frowned. "What I do with my life isn't your business." But my words were shaky because his proximity was driving me crazy. His shirt, buttoned up to the top button and tucked so neatly under a crimson-colored tie, was screaming to be yanked undone. Everything I had wanted to say just slipped from my mind. All the practiced conversations where I leave this building feeling better about the man in front of me and what happened on our date, and perhaps, who knows? Another date organized, maybe.

Gone.

But all my best-laid plans weren't worth anything when the heat from his body was begging me to touch and be touched by him.

Mike seemed to be going through an internal battle, his expression shifting subtly as he fought himself, never taking his eyes from mine.

"What if I want it to be my business?" he finally said.

I shook my head. "I don't understand you. This is already too complicated, and we've only been on one date."

"I know." He turned his head away from me, keeping his arms in place, allowing me a moment to study the stubble on his chin and jawline. "I'm sorry."

"For?"

He looked at me again, and my breath was knocked from my lungs.

"For how I treated you and for making things complicated."

"Why do you fight so hard? We had a connection, didn't we? At least something worth exploring with another date or two. We didn't have to get physical so quickly. I was only responding to your cues, you know. Not that I'm complaining..." I trailed off. The righteousness I had felt drained away when the conflict was so clearly displayed on his face.

"I'm not a good man, Jacob."

Lifting a shoulder, I shrugged. "I don't see it. I think you act like an asshole so no one will get close to you." His stare was piercing, and I couldn't look away, trying to find the words to communicate with him when my mouth was dry at the way he devoured me with his gaze. "We can take it slow," I offered, lifting a hand as though to touch him but dropping it back to my side before making contact. Mike followed the movement with his eyes. "I think maybe you need someone in your life, even if it's not me long term. If I can help you get past whatever is holding you back, I'll be happy."

Mike looked to be in pain, his face on the border of screwing up, his lip lifted almost into a snarl. "You can't help."

"Won't know until we try. What do we have to lose?"

He simply watched me again, and I wanted to know what he wasn't saying because it certainly felt like he *wasn't* saying much more than he was.

"I'm going to regret this," Mike mumbled, and I was about to ask what when his lips met mine. There was no sweet lead-up, no teasing of lips on lips, and enjoying the taste of each other. The kiss was fueled by desperation, passion, and maybe a touch of anger as if to say *is this what you wanted?*

God, yes.

Mike dominated the kiss as he closed the space between us, backing me against the wall until all I could feel was the heat from his body pressed against mine. I tried to return the passion, but Mike took over, running his fingers through my hair before grabbing a handful and yanking my head back, licking up my neck and throat as I groaned.

It was back, the magnetic pull between us—two opposites unable to stay apart—and when he would pull away slightly, I would grab his arms and tug him straight back next to me, needing more of him. The kiss was a reflection of us, and it was driven by power, passion, and an inkling of hesitation that crept through in the way his fingers danced up my arm, a gentle touch compared to his grip on my hair.

"Fuck, Mike..." I moaned as he grabbed my cock

through my pants, finding the outline of my length with his fingers and gripping *hard.* When I whimpered as his grip increased, he chuckled, dark and full of promises. I reached up, running my hands down his chest.

Mike hissed in pain and recoiled from my touch.

Fuck, not again.

No, this was different.

Mike was trying to protect his chest from touch without touching it himself, hunched over, his lips, slightly swollen from our making out, were pressed together, and his eyes squeezed shut.

"Oh shit. I'm sorry, are you hurt?"

"It's nothing,"

"Doesn't seem like nothing," I said, and as I reached an arm up to touch him, he snatched at my wrist lightning fast and with an intense glare. My brows pulled together in a frown. "Are we going to go backward this soon?"

Mike sighed, patting over his chest tenderly and straightening his back. He watched me again for a moment, spending more time in his head deciding what he wanted to do. I was about to say something when he started undoing his cufflink on his left wrist, and I tried not to gasp out loud as he rolled the sleeve up to expose his arm.

The scars I had seen glimpses of on his wrist wound all the way up his arm, angry and red, weaving and passing around his limb and, I'm guessing, continuing over his shoulder.

"When my ex and I split up…" Mike whispered, rolling down the sleeve quickly, "… he left me with these."

"Mike…"

"I don't want to hurt you."

"*You* don't want to hurt *me?* Fuck, Mike, I would've thought you'd be more afraid of me hurting *you* after going through…" I trailed off, reaching out to touch his arm over his shirt, unable to feel the scars through the fabric, "… going through whatever caused this."

Mike simply shook his head, and I watched as he bent down to retrieve the cardboard roll, discarded and forgotten, from the floor. He slapped his hand against the control panel again, and the lift whirred into life, continuing its journey upward.

I huffed out a breath. "You've been through hell, and all you're worried about is hurting me." The pieces of this man were starting to come together, and the more he wanted to protect me from himself, the more I wanted to protect him from the world. "You must be an angel or something."

Mike's responding scoff was only half-filled with humor. "Something like that."

As the elevator voice announced our arrival, I grabbed Mike's hand, letting go when he turned back to face me. "Does this mean we're going on another date?"

He searched my face, pausing long enough to make me uncomfortable in my skin. "Yes."

"Good." I smiled, lowering my voice. "This time, you can suck *my* cock before you leave."

A growl emanated from low in Mike's throat, and I swallowed heavily. "Be careful there, Jacob..." he whispered, leaning into me under the pretense of brushing imaginary fluff from my shoulder, "... I might be more than you can handle in that department."

The doors slid closed as he winked at me, a glimpse at the man he portrays on the outside and perhaps wishes he could be all the time.

I was simply thankful I had the elevator to myself, so the erection straining against the fabric of my pants wasn't so damn obvious.

CHAPTER
8

MIKE

Three days of hoping this feeling would pass. This need that seemed to overrun my thoughts since meeting Jacob. But it didn't pass. If anything, it got stronger, and that made me nervous.

Frank strode into my office without knocking, and the huge grin on his smug face told me he was in a shit-stirring mood as if he was ever in any other mood.

"Who's the blondie you were eye-fucking the other day?"

My eyes widened for a split second before I managed to keep my expression neutral, but it was too late. Frank had seen the reaction and was already chuckling as he sat across from me, leaning his forearms on my desk.

There was no point in lying.

"Macintyre's son."

Frank whistled in appreciation. "Damn, Mike, I thought I was the only one who fucked within the business."

"*Used to*, you mean?"

His grin was no less smug at my retort. In fact, it widened when he thought of Charlotte and tossed a glance out the window that overlooked the city as though he could see her working in her office three blocks away. "You know what I meant."

"We're not fucking, and it's not within the business. I don't go around fucking my employees."

Frank held his hands up. "Fair call. But why not? With the fucking, I mean. He was cute and judging by the growing bulge in his pants when you were whispering in his ear, he wants you."

I growled. "Why were you looking?"

"Don't get territorial with me, Mike. I'm the one asking questions here." When I didn't answer, Frank sighed and leaned back in the chair, it squeaking in protest to his weight. "Listen, Mike, I know you bonded, and I know it was severed. The scars speak for themselves." I moved to roll my sleeves even though they were already down, and Frank watched the movement. "We've known each other for a long time, before Earth, and have worked together here for over a decade. Don't you think it's about time you told me what happened?"

I watched him without speaking. Frank had

never asked before, and although he was an arrogant son of a bitch, he did care about those close to him in his own way. I assumed he hadn't asked previously through some level of respect for my privacy, knowing if I wanted to tell him, I would. But it had been so long now that telling him would feel more like a betrayal than keeping it a secret. I was young and stupid enough to bond with someone I didn't know as well as I thought I did, and in doing so, I created a monster, corrupting Tate until he was as bad as the very demons I had come to Earth to get away from.

How do I tell Frank I'm afraid of doing it again?

When I was silent for too long, Frank continued, "Fine, don't tell me yet, but when you want to, you can." He was met with more silence. This time because I didn't know what to say, as an offering for an open conversation wasn't exactly his style. Perhaps his human partner, Charlotte, really had changed him. "But whatever it was, you need to stop punishing yourself. You haven't dated in ages. Why not give yourself a break?"

"Because I don't want to hurt him."

Frank chuckled. "So work one out before you fuck him," he said, miming jacking off with his fist. "Get some of the pent-up energy out so you have more control of your demon."

"That's not what I meant…"

Frank's cell rang, and he threw me a wink and a

smirk as he picked up the call and left my office.

How could I admit I had lost the one outlet I had for controlling my demon? What if I ended up being worse for Jacob than I was for Tate?

I wanted Jacob in a way I hadn't wanted anyone in a long time, and while I wished Frank were right and I owed myself a break, forgiving myself was turning out to be an impossible task.

Jacob insisted it was his turn to choose the venue for dinner, and while my lip lifted into almost a snarl, he simply chuckled as I mumbled, "I didn't know we were taking turns." His laughter waivered at the implication between the lines. Pulling up to a stoplight, I took the chance to stare him down hard. I loved the way he seemed to unravel under my gaze, and since our rendezvous in the elevator, I'd been thinking about little else apart from getting him in bed.

That and Tate. I'd successfully pushed him from my mind for years, where he only haunted the darkest recesses of my memory I tried my best to ignore. But he was back, larger than life as always, and reminding me of what I had done to him when we bonded and the monster I'd created.

These conflicting desires, coupled with the fact I had recently lost my most effective outlet to satiate my demon, and I wasn't sure if I wanted to get involved with Jacob.

But for the first time in a long time, my demon was winning. When I watched Jacob do almost anything from the way he slid out of his seat to get out of my car to the almost dance-like motion with which he turned to face me, waiting for me to meet him after I closed my car door, inside, I was screaming to take him. I was afraid I wouldn't be gentle, as one should be for the first time with a new partner who was more than a one-night stand. But maybe he didn't want me to be gentle, maybe the way he ground against my touch in the elevator and whimpered as he grew hard told me he desired a rough touch. He wanted to be dominated, and to have the pleasure in submission.

I could give that to him.

Breathing in the crisp night air deeply through my nose, I smiled as I approached him, sliding my arm around his waist and guiding him toward the door of the bistro he had chosen. It was certainly a lot more casual and low-key than my choice of restaurant, and when we stepped inside, it was apparent I was the only one in a suit, but it wasn't a bad place. The lighting was warm but low, and the music—country, not my first choice—played softly enough I could tune it out as background noise.

Jacob told me this place had the best steaks in the city, maybe even in the state. I chuckled and pulled him against me as we were led to our table, my stomach growling, making Jacob laugh, reaching over to pat my stomach and pausing just long enough to trail his fingers over the outline of my abs.

A growl rumbled through my throat at his touch. I think he put it down to another complaint by my empty stomach.

As we sat, I said, "Why this place in particular?"

"Other than the steaks?"

Smirking, I nodded. "Yes, other than the steaks."

"I thought it might help you relax, although…" he looked around pointedly, "… you're slightly overdressed."

"Maybe everyone else is underdressed."

Jacob glanced at his own outfit—a white linen shirt, sleeves rolled up to reveal arms with more muscle than I was expecting, but then again, if he's working on cars in his free time, it shouldn't surprise me, and jeans. When he looked back at me, he was grinning, and I realized I had a slight smile almost permanently fixed on my face simply because I was looking at him. "Na, I think it's you," he joked.

"Right," I said, smirking and picking up my menu. "Do I even need to look at it or shall I just get the steak?"

"Just get the steak, biggest one they have. My treat."

"That's not how this works."

"Oh?" His eyebrow arched as I watched his face while he studied the drinks menu. "Are you going to make some thinly-veiled comment about *taking turns* again, or are you going to just let me get you dinner?"

"Would you rather I made a more direct comment?"

"Later, sugar daddy. I'm thinking about drinks."

I barked out a laugh which had him chuckling too. What was happening to me? I almost felt relaxed. It wasn't until I realized my shoulders had slumped slightly and I leaned forward to read the back of his menu that it occurred to me how long it had been since I had truly relaxed. Isn't this what I came to Earth for? To find this inner peace within me and live as a human? I'd been on edge denying my demon for so long, was freedom found in allowing it to come through, just a little bit?

That seemed to be Frank's theory. At least, that's how it appeared he lived.

Was I seriously considering taking a page out of Frank's book? If he found out, I'd never live it down.

Jacob ordered a glass of wine for me and a whiskey for himself from the waitress. Then we waited as the menus were removed, my arms crossed, leaning on the table, and Jacob with his chin resting in his palms, and we stared at each other for a moment. There was a hint of amusement in his hazel eyes, glinting with mischief and curiosity. When he was out of the workplace and away from the world he didn't feel comfortable in, he relaxed entirely, and he became even more spellbinding to me, and I wanted that. I craved that inner calm, the ability to switch off the outside world and anything happening in business or that happened in my past and simply focus on the moment.

Here, in this odd diner with conflicting décor on the walls, everything from records to a long-horn bull skull and decorative glass vases, with Jacob, I almost grasped it. And I found myself wondering if he would help me get there and if being with him would allow me the peace I had sought for so long.

There wasn't an uncomfortable silence as we simply watched each other, Jacob's face telling a tale as his expressions changed. When our drinks were delivered, neither of us had spoken, and a smirk was playing on the corner of his lips.

When he lifted his middle and forefingers and pressed them to his temple, he squinted at me, and I broke first, laughing out loud.

It sounded strange. I hadn't done more than a chuckle in a while.

"What are you doing?"

Jacob hummed before dropping his fingers. "Trying to read your mind."

"I thought we were having a romantic moment gazing into each other's eyes?"

"We were, but I like it when you laugh."

In response, I huffed out a note of amusement before taking a sip. The wine was cheap, but it would do. I'm not sure when I became such a snob for wine and restaurants, but I suspect it was around the time I made my first million. I'd say Jacob grounded me, but I didn't need grounding. I was more than aware enough of my flaws.

Perhaps what I needed was someone to show me how to enjoy the moment.

The conversation flowed as dinner was served and subsequently devoured. It was a pretty damn delicious steak, slightly overcooked for my liking, but otherwise, pretty good. Jacob appeared smug when I made sounds of appreciation as I ate, and my stubborn streak forbade me from confessing he may have been right about this place.

The bar became more crowded, and a makeshift dance floor had appeared. Hardly a nightclub, but simply by moving some empty tables to the side it allowed people to move around to the music, which had increased in volume, if they wished.

Everyone was relaxed and content. The feel of it permeated the entire place, and it was infectious to be around.

I'm not one much for signs. Whether God leaves signs for humans or not, I couldn't say for sure, but if He does, I can't imagine He would do the same for demons. Technically, we shouldn't even be on Earth, right?

So when that song started playing, it must have been only a coincidence.

Van Morrison's "Into the Mystic."

I couldn't even tell you what it is about the song that affected me so much, but something about it— the tone, the lyrics, and the voice—reached into a part of me I wished I could capture forever.

"What's wrong?" Jacob asked.

I'd been staring off into the distance. "Nothing, I just... love this song."

"Want to dance?"

Chuckling, I shook my head. "I don't dance."

"Can't or won't?"

"Take your pick."

Jacob ignored my protests and stood, holding his hand out. He had that smile again of mischief, and holding back the urge to roll my eyes like a petulant child, I took his hand, engulfing it in mine and allowing him to lead me to the small area with a handful of other dancers. His body fit perfectly against mine, and I took one of his hands, letting my other drape around his waist as he touched my shoulder. We were back to staring at each other, turning in slow circles. My heart was thumping against the inside of my chest, and I'm certain Jacob would have been able to feel it under his fingers. Everything this music stirred in me was coming to the surface, and I couldn't tear my gaze from the man I held in my arms.

I'd never felt less like a demon than I did in this moment, where it was only him and me.

As Van Morrison sang us out of a dance, we stopped, still holding each other, and I tightened my grip, not yet ready to let go of Jacob or this feeling.

"Do you want to come back to mine?" I asked.

"Yes," Jacob whispered, his breath hitching as his fingers gripped my shoulder. "Fuck yes, I do."

CHAPTER 9

JACOB

There was no slow build, no hesitancy of standing at the threshold, arms at our sides awkwardly waiting for the other to make the first move. There was, however, a fumbling of keys, which clattered to the floor the second we passed through the doorway, and a front door kicked shut with a little bit too much force, rattling the frame. A small chuckle escaped my lips at this, and Mike smirked as he grabbed me, shoving me further into the apartment toward the bedroom. Mike's hands were on my body, somehow everywhere at once, all over my arms, shoulders, and torso before they'd run down my body and over my ass, lifting me against him as our lips and tongues met in desperation.

I wanted to slow down, to indulge in all the moments leading up to the ultimate pleasure. But

Mike growled whenever I pulled away from him for air and made it clear he was in charge and there would to be no slowing down. There was liberation in that, in letting go and allowing him to take me, and he was so fucking sexy, I wasn't complaining.

Grunting as Mike pushed me against the wall, he made quick work of the buttons on my shirt, folding it back over my shoulders and discarding it to the floor, kicking it away as though it was a weapon and I was going to snatch it up and attempt to redress. I wanted his hands on me, and his palms were hot as he immediately moved down to undo my pants, grazing gently against my abdomen and smirking when I twitched and moaned. My hands shook as I tried to undress Mike with the same stealth he was me, but he was moving so fast in smooth and calculated motions, maneuvring me to his will.

Mike shrugged out of his jacket as I bent to take off my shoes, and when I looked up, he was watching me, a smirk on his face that slowly ebbed away as he started with the buttons on his shirt. Grinning, I shifted slightly until I was on my knees, running my hands up his thighs, teasing him with my fingertips through the fabric.

Now it was my turn to take my time.

Slowly, I unzipped his fly, smirking to myself as he moaned before I had even touched him. Undoing his belt, I went to free his cock, already hard, from his pants when Mike grabbed my hands.

"No," he said. When I met his eyes again, his expression darkened.

"What's wrong?" It was impossible not to let the feeling of dread bubble in my stomach and settle over me. Was he going to reject me again? Was he going to let his fears get the better of him and not allow me this level of closeness?

"I want to pleasure you." I came to my feet as Mike pulled me up. "Let me touch you."

I straightened and stood motionless, unsure of what he wanted me to do. As he continued unbuttoning his shirt, my eyes shot to his, and it was impossible to move my gaze from his and the plethora of emotions that played across his face. I had been so distracted by the prospect of getting his cock in my mouth, I hadn't acknowledged he had begun the process of removing his shirt. The full significance of the move hit me all at once, and I hesitated for a moment, unsure what to say and settling on not saying anything. Mike held my eye contact as he voluntarily shrugged off his shirt in front of me, exposing his body to me and opening himself up in the most vulnerable way.

Now faced with him half-naked before me, I tentatively lifted my hand to touch the scars on his arms, glancing at his face for signs he would shut down again. But Mike was watching me, his gray eyes studying my movements as much as they were filled with pain. There was the smallest flinch and twitch of his shoulder when I placed my fingers against the scar on his wrist, but he didn't pull away. Emboldened, I followed the trail of the scar up his arm. The scar tissue was smoother than the rest of his skin, the hair on his muscular arms interrupted by the movement of the scar running around his body. As I got closer to his shoulder, Mike started to tremble but never took his eyes off my face as I explored his body slowly and tentatively, relishing in him allowing me to finally touch him.

"Jacob…" Mike started but said nothing further, even as I paused my exploration to hold his eye contact for a beat. He had a heavy gauze pad taped to his chest, and I frowned, throwing him a questioning glance. Mike simply shook his head, the movement barely there and accompanied by his eyes squeezing shut for a second. I was awed at him allowing me even this close, given at our first meeting he wouldn't even allow me to see the scars on his wrists, so I decided not to push the matter about whatever he was hiding behind the padding on his chest. Did he get a tattoo removed or something? Something he was desperate for no one to see?

I resolved to ask him about it later.
I needed to make sure he wasn't self-harming.
Perhaps he needed me more than I thought.
The scars traced down his torso, and I glanced up

at his face again for the briefest moment of confirmation before I pulled his pants down, exposing the V-shape of his muscles, guiding my fingers to where I wanted to touch him most.

"Aren't I supposed to be undressing you?" Mike mumbled as his pants fell to his ankles, and I danced my fingers across his thighs. "Touching you?" His words were breathy, catching when I lightly traced my fingertips over his cock, smirking when it jumped at my attention.

"There's plenty of time for that."

The scars continued down his legs, and my heart squeezed in my chest at the pain he must have endured. Who could have done such a thing and why? I can't imagine Mike doing something to deserve such treatment, although it was clear he felt he deserved nothing better.

Kicking his shoes off before stepping out of his pants, Mike grabbed my wrist. "Strip for me." The breathy voice was gone, replaced with something stronger and more commanding. A shudder ran up my spine as I straightened, and when I didn't move immediately, Mike's grip on my wrist increased. "I said... *strip.*"

Nothing about him being naked diminished the power in his voice.

"I'm already half-naked," I whispered.

His eyebrow arched, and a shadow of a smile played along his lips. "It's not enough."

Mike strode past me, looking back long enough only to make sure I was following before moving toward the bedroom. His steps were strong and purposeful, and I took the chance to admire him from behind—the shape of his shoulders and back, his slender waist and ass, those perfect thighs—none of it was *ruined* by scars. Of course, I would take them away if I could, only because of the pain they represented and what he must have gone through to get them. But his body spoke of strength and resilience, and he moved with a grace I hadn't noticed as prominently while he was in his suits.

When he turned and sat on the edge of his bed, his nakedness was on full display as his cock stood erect, making it impossible for me to hold his eye contact. There was an element of smugness to his face now which made me grin. Being naked and him seeing my reaction to his body brought a swagger to him that only enhanced the appeal of that power and hint of arrogance he displayed while conducting business.

"Strip," he commanded again, and I glanced down, curling my toes against the cool floor and undoing my pants. They were the only item of clothing I had left on, and Mike's smirk grew when he realized I wasn't wearing any underwear. "Commando," Mike commented.

I chuckled. "Always."

His eyebrow quirked. "Good to know."

Sliding my pants down, I stepped out of them and kicked them to the side as he had my shirt earlier.

"Lie down." Mike slid to the side, opening up a space for me to move onto the bed.

The anticipation moved across my skin in slight trembles, and I did as instructed, laying on my back and watching his eyes as he moved over me, the heat from his body almost unbearable. When I lifted a hand to touch his chest again, desperate to feel the hardness of his muscles under my fingers and wanting to memorize every line and shape of his body, that ever-present fear lingered that he may close off from me again, and I wouldn't get another chance.

But Mike grabbed my wrist, pushed my hand back against the pillow next to my head, and gave me a look that made it clear I was to remain as he had silently instructed.

"I want to touch you," I said, and Mike smirked again.

"You're not very good at taking orders."

"You haven't ordered me to do anything."

He grabbed my other wrist, held me against the bed, and pinned me down like a predator. "Stay still. Don't touch me unless I say so. Don't move."

His voice had deepened, darkened, and I sank into the pillows, slightly away from the power he was emanating. "Okay."

He nodded stiffly before the smirk returned, and

he lowered slightly, resting his weight on top of me and hovering his lips above mine. I pouted, trying to sneak a kiss from him, but all I felt was the curve of his lips as he smirked again and moved to run his tongue down my neck, causing me to arch against him. Mike traced his tongue down my body, flicked over my nipple, and dipped into my belly button before he kissed his way down the trail of fine hair from my stomach. I was writhing by this point, desperate to touch him, to grab his head and run my fingers through his hair. Mike gave me one more smirk before he dropped down, took my cock in his hot mouth, and made me cry out.

"Fuck!" As with our entrance to his apartment, there was no waiting, no taking it slow and working up. Mike immediately started moving his head up and down, taking my full length in his mouth before pulling back and tracing his tongue around the head. "Fuck, Mike… *fuck, fuck, fuck.*"

His chuckle was dark, and in one swift motion, he grabbed the back of my thighs, lifted and pushed so my knees bent back, and I was exposed to him. Mike ran his deliciously hot tongue over my hole, and I saw stars. He began to lick and tease before he pushed his tongue inside. I lost control then, reached out and tried to grab at his shoulders, whether to push him away or bring him closer, I wasn't sure.

Dropping my hips, he tongued at my balls before

he ran his tongue up the length of my cock again and sucked hard on the head.

Oh God, if I gave him even an ounce of the pleasure he was giving me, I'd be happy.

Maybe I'd have to work harder next time.

With what felt like little effort, he flipped me over, grabbed my ass and spread me, exposing me to him before tonguing at my hole again. I groaned into the pillow, gripped the bedsheets, and bunched them up under my fingers.

"On your knees," Mike commanded.

I shifted until I was bent over in front of him. Mike kneeled behind me, ran his cock up and down my ass, and teased me with the head, pushing forward as though he was going to penetrate and waiting for me to groan before he pulled away. Mike leaned over to get to the drawer, and I turned my head to watch as he pulled out a bottle of lubricant. When he saw me watching, he smiled in a way that sent a shudder down my spine and made my cock twitch.

Getting back in position behind me, I heard the click of the lid and the wet slick as he lubed up his cock and pumped it a few times with his hand. The cold dribble of the lube on my ass made me jump, and when Mike slid a finger inside me, I groaned. Mike leaned over me, adding a second finger and growling as I moaned louder.

"If it hurts, tell me to stop."

"What if I don't want you to stop?" I panted.

He chuckled, dark and deep. "The safe word is *construction plans.*"

I laughed out loud, the sound hitched and jagged as he continued to maneuver his fingers inside me. "That's the least sexy thing I can think of."

"That's the point." Another growl rumbled through his throat, and he chuckled against my ear. "So when you're begging me to stop, I know you really want it harder."

I whimpered, and Mike moved back, positioning himself behind me again. When he removed his fingers, I felt empty, but I didn't need to wait long. The head of his cock pressed against the entrance to my ass, and I recalled the feel of my lips around it and the intimidating size as he had pushed into my mouth.

I think I might be in trouble.

"You're so fucking tight, Jacob," Mike muttered, and the grip of his left hand on my hip increased.

He pushed forward with a small jolt and broke through the resistance, and I cried out. He filled me so deliciously and waited a beat for the safe word which wasn't going to come as he pushed in further, slow and steady until he was fully sheathed inside me. My cock twitched, desperate for attention, but I was under Mike's control and knew I wasn't to touch myself until I had his permission. He wasn't moving, simply gripping my hips with both hands and staying still inside me, every twitch of his cock sending a jolt of pleasure through me.

"Please," I whimpered after a while. "Fuck me, please."

His only response was a growl before he started moving, thrusting in and out in steady, practiced motions. Every thrust was a world of sensations and pleasure, and I didn't bother trying to keep quiet as he hit the right spot inside me, almost making me come on the spot.

Something came over him, and as his thrusts increased in speed and power, I moaned anew, taking everything he had to give. Mike was grunting with each thrust, the sounds of our fucking punctuating our joint moans.

He went harder, and I cried out as he leaned over me, changing the angle inside me hitting a new sensitive spot. Mike's hands came around my neck briefly before he moved his fingers into my mouth, holding my lips open as he fucked me ruthlessly. I moaned, and Mike growled again, but something was different this time. It was darker, gravellier, and harsher in tone.

"God..." I managed to push the word out around his fingers.

"God isn't making you feel this way." He growled, making me whimper as he hit a new speed. "*I am.*"

CHAPTER 10

MIKE

While I didn't feel as though I was going to lose control of my demon, being completely inside Jacob's tight ass tested my control. Every delicious little *uh-uh-uh* sound he made as I fucked him, gripped his hips, or stuck my fingers into his mouth, holding him in place and making him take everything I had to give was liberating.

My demon wanted more.

Pulling out of Jacob's ass, he moaned as I moved him around, pushed him onto his back, crawled over him, and planted a kiss on his mouth, forcing his lips open with my tongue.

"Spread your ass for me," I commanded.

Jacob mumbled another obscenity, his face flushed with pleasure as he did as instructed. Jacob's hands trembled slightly as I shifted, leaning over him and sliding my cock into his ass. Jacob squeezed his eyes shut as I bottomed out inside him, and with one hand on the back of his head, I nestled his face against the crook of my neck and used the other hand to guide his hips, fucking him.

"Bite me," I hissed out, increasing the grip on his blond locks and pressing his face against me.

What was I doing?

I was losing control.

Jacob hesitated for a moment, and as he opened his mouth and his teeth came into contact with my skin, I groaned, and my eyes returned to their natural yellow. My thrusts increased, and I changed the angle, tilting slightly so I was thrusting against his prostate, reveling in how the pitch of his moans changed. When he moaned, I pushed his face further against my neck.

"Bite me!"

What am I doing!

I couldn't help it.

I needed the pain, the meeting of pleasure and the agony of blood being drawn because Jacob had seen me at my most vulnerable. He had brought out a side of me I wanted so desperately to be the real thing. A part of me I would give anything to have as all that I am instead of being a demon in a human disguise. So, my demon was fighting back at the worst time and, in the worst way, demanding pain when all I wanted was the pleasure.

Jacob bit lightly at first, increasing in pleasure when I demanded, *"More!"* and twisted my fingers into his hair. I snarled as he broke the skin. He shifted, unsure if he had hurt me, but I kept my grip on the back of his head and held him there, muttering, *"Yes..."*

With another few harsh thrusts, Jacob cried out. I felt him near his peak, and I removed my hand from his hip long enough to pump his cock a few times until his cum shot up against his abs as I held him close to me. Jacob continued to moan as he trembled through his orgasm.

I was so close, and with a few final thrusts, I came, gripping his hips and hair harder than I would have liked and made him whimper as I released inside his tight ass.

As I came down from my orgasm, Jacob's tongue touched the droplets of blood on my neck, and I squeezed my eyes shut in panic as the yellow of my natural eyes took over, and a growl shuddered through my chest. My mind's eye flashed an image of Tate, his face as clear as I could remember seeing in a long time.

Only this wasn't a memory.

This was present day.

I was seeing him as he was now, at the exact moment that Jacob tasted my blood and started the first stage of bonding. The act that I had sworn never to take again, and in a moment of weakness, I had let my demon take over more than I should, more than I had in years, as it demanded a connection caused by a confusion of feelings within me. A mixture of my human feelings and experiencing things I had long thought I wasn't capable of, and my demon demanded something closer, something more instinctual.

A bond.

To possess.

To claim.

When my blood hit Jacob's tongue, when he swallowed and it spilled into his body, fusing with his blood and marking him as mine, Tate felt it. As my severed partner, there were remnants of a connection that I would never be able to get rid of.

And at that moment, Tate knew where I was, who I was with, and what we were doing.

He knew about Jacob.

He *knew.*

Jacob was affectionate after, and I cared for him, holding him close as he sighed with contentment. I blinked rapidly until I knew my eyes were clear of all signs of yellow before returning his warm gaze, and it was hard not to smile at the way he looked at me. Until it hit me that I didn't deserve to be looked at like that and didn't deserve his affection.

He didn't even know what we'd done, what *I'd* done.

There was a moment of concern when Jacob touched his fingertips to the blood on my neck, wiping it away with such tenderness I almost snatched at his hand to keep him from touching me.

What the fuck was wrong with me? I had tried so hard for so long not to get too close to anyone, and in a moment of absolute weakness, I had started a fucking bond.

It wasn't done—the bond was only complete if we repeated the act.

I couldn't let that happen. If I did it once, I couldn't trust myself to be strong enough not to do it again. Jacob wouldn't notice any difference this time—any behavioral or physical changes wouldn't occur until after the bonding was complete. I could stop seeing Jacob, push him out of my life and heart, and he would be safer away from me.

After a shower together, where I took my time to soap up and wash Jacob, knowing it would be the last time I got to touch him, we went to bed. He was asleep quickly, nestling into me and wrapping an arm around my chest as I held him close to me. I ignored the stinging pain from the weight of his arm on my chest wound under the dressing. If anything,

I deserved it.

Sleep didn't come as quickly for me, and the silence of the night haunted me, left only with my thoughts, reminding me I had once again destroyed an innocent life.

The door to my ground-floor apartment crashed open, and I looked up from the plans spread across my home office desk. I'd only been on Earth a handful of years, and my business was new, having just finished the education I needed to move forward.

Standing on shaky legs, I averted my gaze from the front door for as long as I could. I knew he would get angry if I didn't look at him, but there was no fear of physical aggression. I was a demon, and Tate, despite being bonded, was only human, and his strength was no match for mine.

When I raised my gaze to his, I immediately took a step back.

"Thomas…"

"Don't call me that, you know I go by Tate now."

I shook my head. Of course, he would argue that point like that was the most important thing when he was standing before me, covered in blood. "What did you do?"

His eyes lit up, flashing with the yellow of demonic power for a moment before being consumed with enthusiasm. "You should have seen it, lover. Dad needed some information, and he didn't ask me... he didn't need to. But I knew I could get the guy to talk."

I squeezed my eyes shut. This wasn't the first time I'd been faced with the reality of what Tate was capable of, and I only had myself to blame. He was dark and charming when we met, and I couldn't quite admit to myself that there was more to him than I had seen when I fell for him.

"What did you do?" I asked, the words muffled behind my hands as I ran them down my face.

Tate laughed. "How much detail do you want? I let him see my eyes. The yellow flashes can be so powerful in scaring the shit out of people. And the teeth... oh, the teeth are helpful too. Sharper than they used to be, perfect for taking off fingers, and—"

"Enough!"

While he stopped talking, the smirk never left his face, and he approached me, sauntering over while removing his blood-splattered coat and letting it drop to the floor. He wasn't wearing a shirt, and a growl pulled through my throat at the sight of his taut chest muscles. I couldn't move, frozen in place as he stopped in front of me, still smirking, and traced his fingers along my chest and up my arms, pulling my hands from in front of my face.

"Don't tell me you're squeamish about a little blood," he said, lifting my limp hand to his lips and planting a kiss on my palm. "You're the demon, after all." His eyes flashed yellow again, and my stomach churned. He wasn't even trying to keep control of his powers. "Do you want to taste it with me?"

"Did you..." I swallowed, "... kill him?"

"Of course."

My chest ached, and at the same time there was a pull from inside me as my demon awoke. The scent of the stranger's blood in my home and the idea of the violence was awakening a part of me I wasn't yet experienced at controlling.

Tate dropped to his knees and began undoing my pants. I wanted to tell him no, to stop, but the words were lost in my throat as he took my cock into his mouth, working his tongue expertly around the shaft and head. With every flick of his tongue and the way he worked his hands, my demon gained further control until my eyes were blazing yellow, and my skin was turning an inky black. Tate looked up at me, his yellow eyes meeting mine. "There's my demon."

I growled, and he took my cock into his mouth again.

Jolting awake, the warm sensation on my cock was still there. Flinging off the blanket, Jacob was between my legs, smiling coyly as he flicked his tongue across the head of my erect cock, achingly hard in his hands.

I felt my demon stir.

"No." I shifted, pushing Jacob away before sliding across the bed and out of his reach. "No, I can't do this right now. I'm sorry."

The smile dropped, and there was anger and pain in his eyes. "What?" He sat up. "What are you talking about?"

He was naked, as was I, and there was nothing I wanted more than to bend him over again and take him hard until he came from penetration alone. But my dream and memories were so vivid in my mind, merging the images of Tate and Jacob, and I couldn't stand it.

"Nothing," I said, running my hand down my face. "Nothing's going on. I'm sorry."

"This on-again-off-again thing is getting a bit old, Mike."

"I know... I'm sorry." I squeezed my eyes shut. What could I tell him? What I should do was push him away and tell him never to come back, that I was no good, and that fucking him last night had been a mistake.

But I couldn't.

Because I cared about him, and I was weak, a coward.

"What is *going on?*"

I couldn't undo what I had done to Tate, but I wouldn't let anything happen to Jacob.

"Nothing, nothing." I cleared my throat. "I'll take care of it."

CHAPTER
11

TATE

There was no security on the house, and from what I knew of the resident, he didn't need it.

What was the difference between Earl and other demons who had chosen to reside on Earth? Looks, mainly. He was darkness, inside and out, and it practically glowed from him. Even humans who didn't know his true nature were freaked out by him. He simply oozed danger, and he played into it, behaving like the absolute scum he was. What did he have to lose?

The second difference was his age. He was fucking ancient, older than any other demon on Earth's surface as far as I knew. Powerful, strong, and downright fucking *dangerous*.

Exactly what I needed right now.

Earl couldn't hold down steady work on Earth

any more than he could hold down a relationship, and he flitted between the criminal factions, picking up work where he could and stealing when he wanted to. Previously, when I had worked under Emrick—a fallen angel who was brimming with self-righteousness and working toward taking over the city from the underground up—he'd told me Earl had survived for a long time without working by mooching off Frank, a demon who ran a successful architecture business at the rich-bitch end of town. Eventually, Frank had tired of Earl's shit and cut him off, forcing Earl to get his funds elsewhere. He then worked for Emrick for a short while but couldn't be trusted, and more than once, Emrick had tried to send folks Earl's way in an attempt to have him killed.

Accidentally, of course.

Earl was loyal to no one and knew everyone. He was a valuable resource.

Which is why I was here.

He knew I was here too. No matter how quiet I was when I broke in through his kitchen window and made my way through the townhouse, Earl knew I was there. So as I stood behind his armchair, drumming my fingers on the old floral fabric, Earl sighed heavily before speaking, "If Emrick sent you here to kill me, and you fail, I can assure you I'll make a formidable enemy."

I chuckled as the dull blue light of the television

played over both of us, casting our shadows into flickering caricatures, animating us into movements we weren't making, our shadows dancing on the wall behind us. "He didn't. I'm here because I want him dead, too, among other reasons."

"Since you invited yourself into my home, you best explain what these other reasons are."

"Nice place." I smirked. "Who paid for it?"

It was Earl's turn to chuckle, a slow and dark drawl that left the hairs on the back of my neck standing on end. Earl could be a powerful player in the crime world if he wanted to be, but leadership wasn't his type of thing. He preferred to slink along underground, keeping out of sight of everyone he didn't wish to encounter and slipping up only to take what he wanted. He was violent and strong, but only for a price.

"Emrick did," he said, not taking his eyes off the television, not at all threatened by my presence behind him and not feeling as though he needed to turn around and protect himself. "Although he doesn't know quite how much."

"He wasn't quite as on top of missing merchandise as he thought he was, right?"

The pause was heavy this time, not his usual lazy response. He was thinking. "No." Earl chose his words carefully, and his long fingers gripped the arm of the chair. "Sometimes his merchandise was easy-picking."

"Sometimes too easy, wouldn't you say?" Earl simply hummed in response, and I imagined he knew where I was going with this. "Almost as though someone was feeding you information, hmm?"

I could hear the smile on the edge of his voice. "It was you then."

"Yes." One of the many seeds I'd planted while I had worked for Emrick. I was always planning on getting rid of him, and since my last attempt didn't work as planned, I had backup now. Those who owed me because of help I'd given them over the years were now being gathered.

It had been years since someone had the guts to storm Emrick's base—the club, Urban—but that was all going to change soon. People here had no loyalty. And demons? Even less so. All they needed was the promise of reward and bloodshed, drugs or money, and they were as pliable as pawns. The bottom-feeders who weren't strong or skilled enough to be under Emrick's direct employ were now under mine. Enough of them together could do a lot of damage. But really, the only one I needed to take down was Emrick. Once he fell, his empire would topple.

That is, of course, if there wasn't someone like me to hold together the pieces. Then the business would be back in the Murphy family, in my hands, where it should have been all along. I had to give Emrick credit for expanding and solidifying the business as quickly and thoroughly as he did. But he was simply a tool to my end game.

Until Mike started a new bond.

I would bring Emrick down later, but getting the revenge I wanted on Mike? Two birds with one stone as it were. The opportunity was too sweet to pass up.

Earl was making noises again, as though he was constantly rolling his tongue around in his mouth, feeling out and choosing each word before he spoke. "What, pray tell, did Emrick do to piss you off?"

"Emrick took what was rightfully mine. The business, all of it, should have been mine and mine alone." I sighed and recommenced drumming my fingers on the back of the chair. "I knew eventually I'd need certain beings on my side."

Earl unfolded himself from the chair to stand and turned to face me. I didn't flinch, although I would admit only to myself that it was a herculean effort not to. Earl's head almost scraped the ceiling, and his arms, too long for his body, fell to his sides. My grip on the chair increased, and when he noticed the slight movement, he smirked, a lazy lift of his lips to reveal uneven teeth. When he reached up to rub his chin, his eyes flashed with anger, a hint of yellow as his smirk turned into a scowl.

"Don't think for a moment you own me, child." He hissed in that same slow tone but edged with a clear threat that permeated the air between us. "It was your choice to leak information to me so I could make some extra cash, I didn't ask you, and therefore, I owe you *nothing.*" I held his gaze, saying nothing as he continued, "And if you expect me to go after *Emrick*, then my regular price just tripled."

"You leave Emrick to me. Something else has come up that caught my interest. Unexpected, but gives me the chance for a bit of extra fun before I go to take my business back."

"What?" The question was a challenge.

"I want you to bring my sister to me."

Whatever Earl was expecting me to say, it wasn't that. "Why do you need me?"

"She's with a demon, and honestly, I just can't be fucked dealing with that shit now. You can take her from under his nose with barely any effort."

He lifted a large shoulder, and I took that to be an agreement.

Nikki was my little sister, whom my father, Mitch Murphy, had doted on right up until he was murdered. He had kept my dear sister in the dark about the true nature of his business, and for the longest time, she believed him to be an upstanding citizen in the community. Even when that illusion was snatched away, she continued to seek out his killer in her spare time, although with less enthusiasm than she did years ago when she had believed him to be a good man.

He treated me like hell and her as an angel.

My revenge on my sister took a back seat while I was working underneath Emrick, biding my time, letting him do what he did best—build up the empire—while I planted seeds of doubt in his leadership which would eventually flourish enough to bring him down. Then I would be waiting to take back what was mine—my father's business that Emrick had stolen.

But that hadn't gone quite to plan, and I had returned underground, taking a couple of months to rally those I could trust to follow me blindly against him. Emrick was strong, within the business and without, and I would need backup if I were to go after him. I was a patient man and had waited over a decade for what was rightfully mine, and with the new and exciting development, taking down Emrick had been moved to a back burner to my new plan.

Because my ex-lover, my severed partner, Mike, had done what I thought he never would.

He started another bond.

I had seen the flash of faces, of flesh on flesh when blood met saliva, and he took the first step for another human-demon bond. Fuck, I didn't think he had it in him. Mike was so convinced all my darkness and everything that made me who I was,

was his fault because of the bonding. The truth was I had taken the strength he offered and used it to become the best or worse—depending on who you were asking—version of myself.

I genuinely thought he would stay away from bonding again, but evidently, I'd been wrong.

So now I was faced with a wonderful opportunity. Before I took down Emrick, I could torture the two people I hated most in the world—Nikki and Mike.

Nikki, for being the apple of my father's eye, who saved all his violence and cruelty for me.

And Mike, for abandoning me, giving me the power and then hating me when I used it, being a coward, and not at all the demon I thought he was. He'd given me these powers, the strength and life force of a demon, and then treated me as though I'd been poisoned when he *was* the poison, and I was the best combination of human and demon and simply used it to my benefit.

If he weren't so weak, he would have used it too, and we could have been a hell of a pair. Instead, I was subjected to the pain and lifelong scars of a severed bond because he couldn't stand the sight of me and was so desperate to get away from what I was to him—a reminder that he was still a demon and had made me so—that he would subject us both to that pain.

Earl could grab Nikki and keep her until I was

ready and maybe make a little extra trouble for Emrick while he was at it and send Nikki's demon lover to him instead of me.

And I would find Mike's new lover boy and torture Mike by taking his life in front of him.

Then I'd kill Mike too.

CHAPTER 12

MIKE

Ray and Ilsa. They'd hate the term bounty hunters, but that was essentially the reputation they had earned themselves. A demon and her human-bonded mate used their time, connections, and skills to track down demons who are new to life on Earth and perhaps haven't quite learned the rules of a socially acceptable existence yet.

Or didn't care.

I was almost certain Ilsa had been in touch with the werewolf community. Ray wouldn't be able to get within thirty feet of them before they'd attack her. Ray let her demonic instincts run her, and it was only her human partner, Ilsa, who kept her in check. But Ray had done something different. While she'd come to Earth intent on causing chaos and destruction, using her twisted logic to convince herself she was doing the right thing by humans and God, she'd changed.

She *learned.*

Demons weren't good at learning the error of our ways, which is why so many who stayed on Earth were involved in the underground crime circuit. It was in our nature, and criminal activity allowed us to be who our instincts wanted us to be.

Ilsa was convinced that more demons could learn to function *with* humans if only they had the right guidance. Something the weres were not convinced of, but they must have agreed to give her at least a bit of space, especially with the lower-end offenders. Because these women had gotten themselves a reputation, and they were good at what they did.

But there was something else I needed them for, something they were equally as good at, although didn't want to make a business from it.

Tracking and security.

Both of which I needed right now.

Because Tate *knew.*

I had seen his face in my mind the second Jacob's tongue had touched my blood.

Fuck. I was so fucking *stupid* to let that happen. Caught up in the moment with Jacob, who made me feel things I had long since forgotten what it was like to experience, and fueled by these emotions, my demon had demanded the bond.

Now, Tate *knew* I had started another bonding. Although our bond was severed, there would always be a thin connection, a tiny rope binding us together across any distance, and he would feel a new bonding of mine as I would if *he* ever bonded again.

God help any demon who fell for him as hard as I did.

It was another layer of punishment, for if another bonding began, the severed partner would feel it and feel the pain of loss all over again. I could never truly be rid of Tate—he would always be as much a part of me as I was him. Now, Jacob was potentially in danger. I had no proof that Tate would come for him, but I felt Tate's rage bubbling beneath the surface as it always did, no matter how cool he appeared on the outside. I sensed it spike the second the connection was made between Jacob and me, and if Tate were to act on that rage, I needed to be ready.

So that is how I came to be in my office with Ray and Ilsa in front of me. Ilsa stood, arms crossed over her chest, army pants and boots only adding to the power of her stance, and even without the demon blood running through her, she would be an impressive being. On the other hand, Ray was seated, leaning back obscenely far in the spare chair and bouncing it up and down. She had found the exact spot on the chair's tilt that created a slight squeak, and she was pushing that point over and over again, so our conversation was tainted with the *squeak, squeak, squeak* of the chair. Ilsa did most of the talking while Ray simply watched me, a smirk plastered on her face as though she knew damn well she was being annoying and waiting to see if I would retaliate.

She would be waiting a long time. A demon didn't work with Frank as long as I did without learning to control his patience.

"Tell us about the demon you want protection from," Ilsa said, watching me.

"He's not a demon… he's a human."

"Bonded?"

My lip twitched. "Severed."

Ilsa glanced at Ray, perhaps for guidance. Maybe she didn't know much about bondings being severed, but Ray's interest was piqued. She stopped squeaking the chair and leaned forward, the legs of the chair hitting the floor with a thump. Ray studied me, but I didn't take my eyes off hers and resisted the urge to adjust my shirt sleeves.

She turned to Ilsa. "Even if a human severed their bond with a demon, they retained the additional strength and power."

Ilsa almost smirked. "Oh, sweet. So if I tire of you, I can fuck you off and keep my new strength?"

Ray was on her feet and held the other woman's hips still as she ground her body against Ilsa's.

"You'd be lost without me, sweetheart."

I cleared my throat, and they both glanced at me. Ray giggled and was about to sit down when the door to my office was shoved open, slamming into the rubber doorstop. Both women dropped into defensive poses, and I snarled as Frank stormed his way into my space, slamming the door behind him.

"What the fuck is going on?" He growled.

"You could've knocked, Frank," I grumbled. His intrusion into my office against my direct instructions was another power play, whether he realized it or not. Every day he was testing me, and one day soon, I'd have to put him in his place.

Physically, with force. Remind him who was the older demon.

"Frank?" Ray piped up.

Frank rounded on her, searching her face before her body, a look which elicited a growl from Ilsa, as though trying to figure out if he knew her before finally asking, "Do I know you?"

"No, but your reputation precedes you. I've met Earl."

He huffed something that could've been a chuckle if he weren't so pissed off. He rounded on me. "Do you mind telling me why there's a demon and her bonded human pet in your office?"

"Fuck you!" Ilsa chimed in.

Gritting my teeth, I leaned back in my chair. I'd had no intention of making this a group affair, and

Frank needed to get his goddamn voice down so he didn't attract the attention of the entire fucking office. I told him as much, and while he snarled at me, he nodded and closed the door.

The more this situation escalated, the harder it was to maintain my calm, and Frank's eyes shot to my wrists as I began to play with my sleeves. "Frank," I started, my tongue suddenly feeling too big for my mouth. This was ridiculous. I was a demon, for fuck's sake. I was older, stronger, and more experienced than almost all demons who were currently living in this city, and yet it took only a whisper of Tate to throw me off. Tate knew me more intimately than anyone else, and I had tainted him and destroyed whatever was left of his humanity.

Clearing my throat again, Frank waited patiently while Ilsa and Ray waited with less patience. "My severed partner... Tate. I believe he is going to come after Jacob."

"What makes you think that?" Frank was leaning forward in his chair, his elbows resting on his knees as he watched my eyes.

Fuck, time to admit I was an idiot. "Last night when we were..."

"Fucking each other's brains out?" Frank offered, unable to stop the smirk that played across his lips.

"Right. Well, in the heat of the moment, he bit me, and when he tasted my blood, I saw—"

"Damn, Mike. You don't fuck around. Starting a bonding the first night you're together?"

"I didn't mean to." I pushed the words through gritted teeth. Frank was enjoying this way too much. Because I was the stable one, the sturdy one, and here I was admitting I had done something reckless with a human.

"And you had a vision of... Tate, is it? And now he knows about Jacob?" Frank knew how it worked.

"Right."

"So why would he come after Jacob?"

"Tate is... unstable." At Frank's arched eyebrow, I flexed my hands nervously. This isn't something I had ever planned on admitting to Frank or anyone. "Once we bonded, he got dark, and he enjoyed his newfound strength a little bit too much. He was hurting people and loving it."

"Jesus, Mike. Didn't you have any idea of what he was like before you bonded?"

"I didn't think he was that bad."

Frank scoffed. "Bullshit. Bonding with a demon doesn't make you evil. If he turned into a monster, then he was already one before you bonded."

While I didn't say anything, I shook my head. I wasn't about to have this argument because I'd already had it a thousand times within my mind. No matter how smitten I was with Tate, how new I was to Earth when we got together, or how much he charmed me, I simply couldn't find it within myself to accept that I hadn't seen what sort of person he was before we bonded. The only explanation that made sense to me was that I created him, turned him into the monster, and it was my fault and mine alone.

And now, Jacob was in danger. I could feel it.

"So, you hired these two to track him down?" He waved a hand at Ilsa and Ray. "Why not just ask me?"

"I didn't want to get you involved."

"Too late. I'm involved. Now let me help."

There was a moment where we stared at each other, each of us equally stubborn and fully aware the other wasn't going to bend on the issue. There was a part of me that was touched that Frank wanted to help, but this was my mess, and I didn't expect him to put himself out helping me sort out shit that should never have happened in the first place.

Fuck, I was too old for this shit. I should've known better.

Was I so desperate to leave my demonic influence behind that I fell for the first human who showed me attention and love? At least, what I thought was love.

"Where's Jacob now?" Ilsa asked.

"At mine. He's safe… for now."

"Did you tell him what was going on?"

"That my crazy ex had found out about us and

might be coming after him?" I sighed. "Unfortunately, I had no choice. He was supportive, but I hate that this is happening at all." Hate was barely a strong enough word because self-loathing was fueling me right now.

It turns out self-loathing is good at keeping control of your demon. *Noted.*

"Do you have a photo of Tate?" Ray spoke up.

Nodding, I opened my desk drawer. I had searched my apartment before leaving this morning, and while photographs of us together were almost non-existent, I was sure I had at least one. Locating it, I slid the picture across the desk, and Frank reached for it, scowling when Ray snatched it out from under his hand. She stared at the image for a beat, taking in the white-blond spiked hair and his smile that did not travel to his eyes. When Ray and Ilsa shared a significant look, I spoke up.

"What is it?"

"Someone else has a price on his head."

"Who?"

The women exchanged another look. "Emrick. We didn't know it was the same Tate. We don't kill."

"I'm not asking you to."

"But from what we've heard, this one..." Ilsa tapped the photograph, "... might not leave us with a choice. We can play security guard for you, but he might force our hand."

I didn't want Tate to hurt Jacob, but would I be willing to kill him to stop it? He was still only a human, and a demon killing a human was a one-way ticket back to Hell with no hope of being allowed on the surface again. My mark was already destroyed, and my chest throbbed in memory, so they wouldn't need to take it from me. But if Tate managed to kill me, I wouldn't go back to Hell. I would simply cease to exist.

I had been in control for so long, but the second I saw his face in my mind, everything began to unravel, including my thoughts. Did I still love him somewhere deep inside? Perhaps. But I simply hadn't considered that killing Tate might be the only way to stop him. Having the protection of Ray and Ilsa would be helpful for the short term, but they couldn't spend the rest of their lives watching my apartment, and I couldn't keep Jacob locked up indefinitely, although the idea was tempting.

"Find out what you can from this Emrick," I said.

Ilsa stared hard at me even as Ray stood. "We have no intention of taking on Emrick's job."

"Again, I'm not asking you to. I need to know what Emrick thinks Tate's next move might be or where he might be if I can talk to him..."

"You don't seriously think you can reason with Tate?" Frank stood too.

Slowly, I followed suit, only so I could be eye-to-eye with Frank, and while I expected to find anger there, all I saw was sympathy. I must be a pathetic figure in his eyes for him to have such empathy for me, something Frank is hardly known for.

"We'll find out what we can," Ilsa said, taking Ray's hand and leading her from the office before I could get another word in.

Frank continued to stare at me even as the door clicked behind them. After a moment of silence where you could almost hear the air beating against your eardrums, he said, "Why didn't you tell me earlier? Maybe we could've dealt with this."

"How, Frank? You can't kill him. You're bound by the rules just as I am."

Again the silence and again a moment where we stared at each other. I knew he was thinking of the time I had lost control of my demon and violently killed a handful of men. But I was nothing more than animal at that point, and no matter how many times Frank drilled me about that night, I couldn't tell him how I had ended up hours outside of the city and at that drug lab.

And I hated the idea as much as Frank did that an out-of-control demon was simply another of God's pawns, and those men were destined to die.

But there was a level of comfort in that explanation because it took away some of the guilt. Not all of it, but enough.

So this brought us back to Tate. I knew that one day this would come back to haunt me, and I had tried so hard to stop myself from getting close to another human. Then there was Jacob, leaning against the desk in his father's office, his arms crossed over his chest, eyeing me as though he could see what I was thinking. Physical attraction turned into lust and then morphed into something more when this man had insisted there was something in me worth saving, and he was the one to do it. He had made me feel I was worth caring for, made me laugh for real, and in moments forget I was a demon underneath this skin and think maybe my life on Earth wasn't entirely a lie.

Frank had said nothing because he didn't know what to do any more than I did. Talking to Tate was my only chance, and I simply had to hope there was enough humanity within him to see reason. He hated me for severing the bond and thought because I was a demon, I would approve of his behavior, and maybe we could go on some fucked-up outings together, hunting and hurting innocent people. How disappointed he was to learn the truth—the first demon he'd ever encountered was nothing more than a coward running away from his true nature and had come to Earth not to seek thrills and mess with humans but to live amongst them, and as much as I can be, *be* one of them.

He hated me, and I feared he would take it out on Jacob.

Ray and Ilsa had to be able to help because I

didn't know what else to do.

Ray and Ilsa stopped by shortly afterward to tell me that Emrick—a fallen angel who ran the largest underground crime syndicate in the city—was on his honeymoon. When my eyebrows shot up, Ray snorted. "Yeah, *what the fuck,* right? Whatever. Apparently, he'll be back tomorrow."

"Right. Well, I'm coming with you when you go."

They looked like they were about to argue with me, then thought better of it and simply shrugged and left, promising to be back tomorrow.

Was I crazy to think that I could reason with Tate? That he would leave me with any choice but to kill him? And if he pushed me that far, I would then never be able to see Jacob again. Maybe that was his plan, and when it came time for us to face each other, either my punishment would be death or be torn from another human I had grown to love.

CHAPTER
13

JACOB

It was only after some serious nagging that Mike admitted to me what had him so rattled. Nagging wasn't really my style. I preferred the subtle approach, and if I could, gently guide someone in the direction of making the best decision for them. But that didn't work on Mike, and he'd stayed refutably tight-lipped until I'd annoyed him into telling me by literally following him around as he got ready for work and tugging on his sleeve. I'd won only when his look of worry morphed into amusement before shifting again into frustration, and he'd thrown his arms up and forced me to sit before telling me about his ex.

He didn't give me much, only enough information to know that he was a dangerous man—like I couldn't tell that myself from the scars draped over Mike's body—and had somehow found out we were dating and could be coming after me. Mike said his plan was to find Tate first, but in the meantime, he would hire some security to watch over me. While I wasn't sure I was particularly keen on the idea of having a bodyguard, Mike seemed genuinely disturbed, so I didn't argue.

At Mike's insistence, I'd taken a sick day off work and stayed in his apartment all day under strict instructions to answer the door for *no one*. Mike had an interesting collection of books, and I wasn't much of a reader, but I ran my fingers down the leather-bound spines of some of the oldest appearing books, sliding a few out to take a look. He had volumes on the occult and supernatural creatures, which might make me nervous if they took up too much of his collection. But Mike's collection also included classic literature as well as a few dozen modern murder mysteries from well-known authors and some not. Possibly my favorite find was the ancient-looking encyclopedias, which I'd initially been interested enough to flip through but couldn't concentrate on them and the language style used.

He had no books on cars.

So, I watched television.

Breaking long enough to discover a chin-up bar in Mike's closet and using it for a short while. Then I couldn't get the image out of my mind of his topless form, lifting himself effortlessly, the lines of his muscles on display as he worked out, sweating…

That distracted me for a good while, though it felt distasteful to masturbate in Mike's home while he wasn't there, so I didn't.

Around three o'clock, I decided I would cook him something for dinner. While I expected to find a sad, bachelor refrigerator, much like my own, I was surprised at the array of fresh ingredients available. The picture of Mike was becoming clearer with each revelation, and it all seemed to be solidifying the image I already had of him—someone who was in some sort of self-imposed exile. So, he kept himself busy reading, viewing a large film collection, working out, and cooking elaborate meals, all to distract from the fact that he was alone. Mike had fine taste in music, art, and food, judging by the line of cookbooks on the kitchen counter, but he kept to himself.

Was that purely because of Tate? Perhaps what was happening now was exactly as he feared. I hated the idea he had shut himself away from the world out of fear of an ex who could come in at any moment and destroy him for even daring to have happiness.

Mike was larger than life, a powerful force of a man—intimidating, dark, and incredibly sexy.

Yet all I wanted to do was to protect him and turn this bubble he'd created for himself into a bubble for us both.

Mike strolled through the door around four, closing it and making a point of turning the deadbolt and adding the small security chain before turning. He'd called out as he unlocked the door so I knew it was him. Mike dropped his briefcase by the front door and moved toward me, sniffing the air and arching an eyebrow. I continued to stir the pot, smiling as he came to stand behind me. Mike hesitated and stood for a moment while I simply enjoyed the feel of his presence behind me, watching and protecting me.

"What are you making?"

Tapping the spoon on the side of the pot, I replaced the lid and turned, leaning against the counter. He was so close—his hips inches from mine and our chests almost touching—he leaned forward, looking down at me. When he lifted a hand to my hip, the images of him working out returned to the forefront of my mind, and I placed my palms on his chest. Mike was watching me as though I was going to shatter into a million pieces before his eyes or simply disappear from his life. Whatever front he put on, however arrogant and suave he appeared, it was clear it was mostly bullshit.

"Minestrone."

"From one of my books?"

"Nope, just from here." I tapped my temple, and he smiled delicately, moving his jaw so the hints of gray in his five o'clock shadow caught the light.

"Smells great."

"Thank you." After a moment of silence, I asked. "How was your day?"

Mike barked out a laugh, almost instantly replaced with that look of worry he'd had this morning when he left. "All right. I'm sorting some things out."

I began caressing his chest through his shirt, and Mike hummed, closing his eyes for a moment before watching me again. "Are you sure there's nothing I can do to help?" I asked.

"Nothing. Just be patient for a while as I sort it out." My tongue darted out between my lips as he watched me, and his gaze took on a hungry quality.

"Did you get your security?"

His jaw tensed, and he nodded once. "They'll be watching the place while they can, but they can't be here twenty-four-seven."

"Who are they?"

"Friends."

"Aren't there services you can use or something?"

Mike hesitated. "Tate is a… special case. I need people who understand what he's capable of."

"How did you ever get caught up with someone so dangerous?"

Something in his face changed, a mishmash of emotions passing across his eyes—guilt, regret, sympathy, anger—as if to say *I'm the dangerous one.*

I didn't believe that.

"How long until dinner?" he asked, halting my train of thought.

"Twenty minutes? Give or take."

"Good, time for a shower." Mike shifted to move away from me, and I grabbed his shirt, stepping forward and pressing my body against his. Images of his body had been haunting me all day. I'd had him once, and now I wanted him again. Mike became an animal when we fucked, and I wanted *more.* Because there was freedom in it, and it felt like there was a part of him that he could only let go in those moments. I recalled the feeling of biting him last night, harder and harder as he begged me to do it until his skin broke under my teeth. I'd gasped, guilt filling my throat as I experienced the faint metallic taste of his blood. But then he'd come so hard I could feel the ropes of it shooting inside me as he gripped my hair, keeping my head pressed against the nook of his shoulder.

My cock twitched at the thought. It looked like Mike had a kinky side.

"Care for some company?"

Again, there was a flash of emotions across his face. As I gently dragged my fingers down his chest, coming to rest over the front of his pants and gripping his cock through the fabric, his expression settled. It was dark and hungry, and I shuddered.

Mike answered by grabbing my head, gripping my hair, and tilting my head back so he could claim my mouth with his. Any sense of hesitation he had when he first stood behind me when he came home was gone, and he took control of the kiss, shoving his tongue into my mouth and groaning with me as I gripped his cock harder. He broke the kiss only to guide me to the bathroom and made quick work of removing our clothes, no longer bashful about his scars, it seemed, and desperate only to be naked with me.

A twenty-minute shower turned into forty, and even as we dried each other, Mike was hard, ready to go again.

Dinner was passable, as the integrity of most of the vegetables had been compromised with the additional unplanned cooking time. I had the stove up too high—my fault. Mike didn't care, and apart from the fact I wanted to show him the best of my cooking and only ended up displaying the mediocre, I didn't either.

Mike was a different person when he was comfortable, stripped of his suit, laid back in only sweatpants and a cotton T-shirt, with one arm flung over the back of the leather couch and an invitation for me to slide in next to him. The sound of his heart beating as I rested my head on his chest was soothing. Although the beats were a little faster than they should be, I put that down to his stress over the situation with his ex. I didn't ask what he expected me to do tomorrow and if he wanted me to take another sick day and stay in his apartment again because, right now, tomorrow didn't matter.

We watched *Citizen Kane* because Mike was floored I hadn't seen it.

"We aren't all so cultured, you know," I quipped, loving the feel of his chest as he chuckled.

"I keep forgetting you're a grease monkey at heart."

I laughed. He wasn't wrong.

Tracing the lines of Mike's chest muscles with my fingertips until I could barely keep my eyes open, we moved to the bedroom, and any tiredness I felt evaporated. Mike lay me down on the mattress, and I grabbed his arms when he moved to get off the bed. He chuckled. "I'm just going to turn the main lights off."

"What? You don't have a clapper? I thought you were classy."

Mike laughed as he padded his way to the main room and switched off all the lights on his way back. Then in the dark, he moved to the window and threw open the curtains, bathing the room in a dull glow from the moonlight outside. The lights of the cityscape blinked to their own tune, and I watched the outline of Mike's shape as he moved toward the bed, the mattress sinking under his weight as he sat. He stared out the window, and I moved along the bed, coming up behind him and kneeling, wrapping my arms around his neck and resting my chin on his shoulder. Mike's hand came up and cupped my forearm, squeezing slightly but saying nothing.

"You're worried, aren't you?"

"If he comes for you, I might have no choice but to kill him, and if I do that, I'll go away, and you'll never see me again."

Kill him?

My arms tensed around his shoulders, the confession had come from nowhere, and I swallowed heavily, keeping my emotions in check as I tried to comfort the man I had my arms wrapped around. Was Mike overreacting, or was I not taking this situation seriously enough? I tried to keep my voice steady. "Why would you have to kill him?"

"I know him, and he hates me. I fear he'll try to use you to get to me."

Mike's earlier words echoed in my mind, *even this close is too close.*

"Is this why you didn't want to get close to me?"

"To anyone, yes... one of several reasons."

"What are the other reasons?"

Mike sighed, patting my arm. "It's my fault Tate is how he is. It's my fault."

"I don't see how that's possible. What could you possibly have done to turn him so violently against you?"

He simply shook his head in slow, sad movements and patted my arm again. Each time we talked, I cracked him open a little bit more and pushed through the barriers he had built. I didn't push the topic again, he'd opened up a bit, and that was enough for now. But soon, I would need to question him further. If I were in as much danger as Mike seemed to think I was, I would need to know the full story.

I unwrapped my arms from Mike's neck as he shifted, turning on the mattress to face me. He took my face in his hands, and I marveled at the gentleness of his touch. I knew he was strong and capable of taking control, throwing me down on the mattress, and having his way with me. My cock twitched at the thought, and I held his eye contact. But when he touched me like this—gentle caresses and looks filled with meaning—it was almost too much to take, as if he was baring his soul to me without words.

He kissed me, and his gentle touch lingered for only a moment longer before the desperation took over again. When he growled—God, I loved it when he growled—his fingers snaked through my hair again, a motion I loved every time he did it, and he continued the kiss for a moment longer before breaking it and trailing his tongue down my neck. When I moaned, he hummed his approval. "I love the sounds you make."

"I've been thinking about you all day," I whispered as he kissed my neck and flicked his thumb over my nipple, making me gasp.

"Really?" His voice was dark, seduction dripping through the tone. "Did you touch yourself?"

I chuckled. "No, it felt weird to do so when I was alone in your home."

"You're not alone now, so why don't you touch yourself?"

Mike grabbed my hand and moved it into my lap, guiding me to wrap my fingers around my cock, already hard from his attention on my neck. With his hand around mine, he worked the length, pumping it in my fist while he continued to swirl his tongue along my neck as though the salt on my skin was the best thing he'd ever tasted.

"Were you having dirty thoughts about me?" Mike continued, and I simply groaned. His voice was intoxicating and deeper than normal, each sentence ending with a growl of satisfaction at the sounds I couldn't help from dropping from my lips as he worked my length using my hand. "Were you picturing me inside you? Stretching you with my fingers and then my cock. Were you seeing yourself on your knees, sucking me dry? Or maybe it's thoughts of my mouth around your cock that would get you off?"

"Mike... *fuck...*"

He was taking control of me again, inside and out. He was everywhere at once with his hands and mouth, and I had to close my eyes when the sensations became too much. I was going to come, and although I didn't want to so soon, I couldn't stop it. Mike sensed my orgasm drawing near, and even as I tried to loosen my grip on my cock, he increased it, pumping harder and faster until I cried out, spraying cum over the bedsheets.

Mike growled again. "I should make you lick that up, dirty boy." He traced his thumb across my lips, waiting until I opened my eyes before pushing his thumb into my mouth. "But instead, I'm going to fuck you until you come again. Is that okay?"

"Yes, please, please." I was a mess around him, willing to throw myself at him and let him do whatever he pleased as long as he kept me teetering on the highs I knew he could bring me to.

"Ooh." Mike hummed again, leaning forward to dart his tongue into my mouth, leaving my jaw agape when he moved away before I could continue the kiss. "I do like it when you beg me. Perhaps we could practice that part a bit more?"

"Please, please, please..." I whispered.

The mattress shifted as Mike moved to his knees. "Bend over," he said, that dark tone to his voice taking over again. "Because you beg so good."

CHAPTER
14

JACOB

It wasn't the moonlight that dappled through the clouds, sprinkling over Mike's bed where I lay that woke me. It was something much less pleasant.

A hand slapped over my mouth, and I reached out, slamming my palm on the empty mattress beside me. *Where was Mike?* The moonlight reflected off the light hair and pale face of the figure above me, and he chuckled, a voice too deep for his slender face, while his hand tightened and painfully squeezed my cheeks together. Precious seconds later, the bathroom door crashed open, banged against the doorstop, and the silence in the room was punctuated by Mike's heavy breathing.

The man above me changed his position lightning fast until he was behind me with one arm wrapped around my chest and the other hand pressing something cold and sharp to my throat. He dragged me from the bed, and my nudity only served to increase the feeling of exposure as he placed me between Mike and himself, using the knife to control my movements. My mind was a blur, and I just complied with the dragging and physical commands of the man behind me. Because what else could I do? He had a knife. And beyond that, when I looked at Mike standing on the other side of the bed, his chest heaving and expression laced with thrilling danger, I saw real fear in his eyes.

If Mike was afraid, then I was fucking terrified.

"I wouldn't make any sudden moves, Mike," the man drawled before shifting his hand. "I might get a bit twitchy and cut him up."

"Tate," Mike whispered before swallowing heavily. "*Tate*." When he repeated the name, his voice was stronger and heavier, as though there was something behind it, a driving force making the word sound like a threat. I wanted to bring my hands up and grip the man holding me, to at least feel like I had some control of the situation, even if it was an illusion. But something in Mike's expression made me stop and stand as motionless as I could and put my faith in him to get us out of this situation.

When I saw it, a frown flickered across my face, and for the smallest beat, Mike's gaze traveled to mine.

A trick of the light... it had to be.

In the dull light of the room, I could've sworn Mike's eyes changed, and a flash of yellow crossed over his natural gray as he stared down Tate, not looking directly at me, not even throwing me a glance. I waited for it to happen again, squinting through the semi-darkness and hoping for any hint that I had imagined what I saw. When it happened again, I recoiled in Tate's hold, and he chuckled.

The effect had been supernatural and was gone as quickly as it had come. Once, and I could have dismissed it, but twice, I think I was going crazy. Mike's lip was twisted in what almost looked like regret, and I wanted to ask what was going on when I was harshly reminded of my situation and the blade pressed against my skin.

Mike took a step forward, his expression darkening, and held up his hands when Tate took a step back, the knife cutting into my skin when he changed the angle. I whimpered, hating the sound as it came from me, but the trickle of blood from my neck spiked my fear. "Tate, let him go."

"Turn on the light," Tate said. Mike hesitated before taking a few steps to the side and flicking on a bedside lamp.

"What do you want?"

Tate ignored Mike's question and readjusted his position so he could hold his arm in front of me.

Gasping, I followed the trail of scars up his arm, identical to those on Mike's skin. *What the fuck was going on?* I'd assumed the scars were a result of something Tate had done to Mike, but *matching* scars? I couldn't explain that.

"You see these scars, human?"

Human? Lost in my thoughts, I didn't answer fast enough, and the pressure of the knife increased again. I nodded, choking out a reply. "Yes."

"Mike gave me these scars."

"You gave them to *yourself,*" Mike yelled.

"I never wanted them, lover. It was *your* choice, *your* move to end us and tear us apart." Tate turned his head slightly, speaking directly into my ear while he slowly waved his arm in front of my face, making sure I got a good look at the scars that wrapped around his skin. "He'll do the same to you, you know. He'll make you into a monster, then he'll leave you."

"You were already a monster!"

Tate chuckled at the outburst. Mike's voice was edged with fear rather than anger and an unhealthy dose of desperation. This side of Mike was frightening. I would have much preferred he was a bundle of rage. Hell, it would have even been better to see him get violent against Tate. I don't condone violence, but it would have been less disturbing than the mixture of fear and pain in his features and the twitch of his fingers, full of nervous energy.

"Are you sure about that?" Mike didn't answer Tate's tease, and Tate laughed again. "Which one of us is the monster, Mike? Maybe lover boy deserves to know."

Mike started shaking his head. "Tate, please, don't…"

"Some demon you are. Why don't you just fucking kill me? We both know you have the strength." When Mike didn't answer, Tate continued to laugh. Mike shot me another nervous glance, the anxious flexing of his fingers working double-time, and my mind was reeling. There was tension in the air, as though there was a truth right below the surface I couldn't quite grasp. Tate and Mike seemed to be teetering around something, hints hidden in their stilted conversation that Mike didn't want me to know. The room started to feel uncomfortable, and the cool blade against my skin was almost an afterthought to the discomfort that permeated me. Tate continued to chuckle at Mike's obvious indecision. "No, wait, don't answer because I already know. You won't kill me because you're a fucking *coward*. You've never been anything but a coward."

Something in Mike snapped, and with a roar of rage, he launched forward, and a warm trickle of blood spilled onto my chest as Tate slid the knife across the front of my throat. There was a blur of motion as I was spun around. Mike seemed to move faster than humanly possible, and a bubble of dread opened in my stomach.

A trick of the light. It's dark.

What was going on?

Something wasn't right, and my body was reacting before my mind could comprehend what I'd seen. I was in self-preservation mode, and my arms came up to protect myself after Tate had cut my skin, a warning cut, not deep enough to kill, only enough to prove he could if he wanted to.

How could Mike move so fast?

But not fast enough, evidently.

There were no words from Mike when he realized I'd been cut, only another roar that sent a shiver down my spine, enough to almost shake the walls, and sounded like it was pushed through his vocal cords two tones at once. Automatically, my hands came to my neck as my arms were released, the cut barely enough to draw blood. A move to make a point and nothing else to remind Mike he wasn't the one in control, and neither was I.

Tate twisted out of Mike's reach, taking me with him and turning until I faced him. His hand was on the back of my neck, the tip of the knife pointed at my Adam's apple, pressing painfully when I swallowed against the fear and bile rising in my throat. His fingertips caressed my throat gently, like a lover, his eyes hungry as he flicked the tip of the blade just as softly over the front of my throat. Not cutting, simply reminding me it was there.

My fight-or-flight stopped dead with the action of the blade, and I stilled. I was a jumble of sensations and confusion inside. There was something dark about Mike's expression as he stopped dead, not taking another step after Tate nodded pointedly at the blade. There was something almost inhuman about him, the darkening of his features, the flash of yellow over his eyes I kept trying to tell myself wasn't real.

The first thought I had was that Tate's reference to Mike being a monster may have been more literal than figurative. But that was crazy, right? The only monsters that existed in the world were like the one in front of me with a knife pressed against my skin, the dark people that hurt others. Internally, I begged someone to say something to clear these thoughts from my mind, anything to tell me that I was crazy and was simply on edge because my life was being threatened.

Closer to the window, Tate's face became clearer. He shot a warning look at Mike when he growled again, shifting the knife to ensure his message was clear. Was he going to kill me in front of Mike? Bleed me out as some sort of punishment for whatever went down between them? With a twitch of his lips, they curled into a smirk, and Tate held my eye contact.

Then his eyes changed.

This was no trick of the light.

His eyes were yellow—a bright glowing yellow that was *definitely* inhuman with black cat-like slits for irises. I couldn't move, frozen on the spot in fear as his fingernails dug into the back of my neck and the tip of the blade pressed harder against my throat. Without words, he was telling me to *look, look at what I am.* I wanted to be the sort of person who took action, who found themselves in a life-or-death situation and took control to be the action hero who, with a sudden burst of energy and skill, saved the day. But instead, I stayed with my arms useless by my sides, staring into the yellow eyes of the devil in front of me.

"No!"

Mike's shout broke the trance, and when the front door burst open, Tate shoved me away from him, moving to the window even as two sets of feet stormed toward him. He looked back at me, taking a purposeful moment to hold my eye contact, yellow meeting my hazel. Inhuman meeting human.

I thought he said, "Don't trust him," but I couldn't be sure. I dropped to the floor as I was shoved again to the side and looked up as Tate disappeared out the window, pursued by a woman with bright red hair down the fire escape as another woman turned to me, holding out a hand. I didn't take it, and she tossed a glance at Mike before reaching down and grabbing my shoulders, pulling me to my feet with strength that didn't match her stature.

Mike came up behind me, and I leaned against him, staring at the floor and unable to wrap my mind around what I had seen. When there were this many thoughts in my head, it was impossible to pin one down, and everything was a blur.

"Ilsa, what the fuck? Where were you? How did he get in?" Mike raged, directing the question at the woman in front of me, military, by the looks of her, and I assumed she was the security Mike had arranged.

"He killed your doorman."

"Peter?"

She nodded solemnly. "I'm sorry, we just got back and came upstairs as soon as we saw what Tate had done."

"Good thing I gave you a pass to my suite," Mike said, his voice hollow.

Ilsa's lip twitched. "We would have broken the door down if we had to. Now..." she paused, looking at me and waiting until I met her eyes—a deep brown, hard, but full of sympathy. "Are you okay?"

"Yeah," I said, my voice felt gravelly like I hadn't spoken in days. I cleared my throat, standing up straight and taking my weight from Mike with the same motion. "Yeah, I'm fine."

"You saw his eyes, didn't you?"

Her voice fleshed out the sympathy in her face, and I shook my head, started to nod, then shook again. "I don't know what I saw."

She shared a significant look with Mike. "I think you two have some talking to do." She moved to leave. "I'm going to follow Ray… see if she caught up with Tate."

"What will she do if she catches up with him?" Mike asked.

Ilsa frowned. "She won't kill him if that's what you're asking. We'll incapacitate him, then call you."

Mike nodded, and his fingers flexed against my upper arms when he held me as if he were to let me go, I would collapse to the floor. Maybe I would. I was still trying to comprehend everything I had seen. It had all happened so quickly, and I could barely process what was real and what wasn't.

Those yellow eyes of Tate's—*those were real.*

The speed Mike had moved with as he came to save me—*was real.*

Mike's eyes shifting to yellow too.

Please, someone, tell me that *wasn't real.*

Mike didn't say a word as Ilsa left, moved silently across the room to close the window, flicked the lock shut, and pulled the curtains closed. His hands remained gripping the fabric, his back to me as he stood for a moment, his shoulders shaking. With anger, fear, or tears, I couldn't tell, and I was too numb to find out. So, I left him to his moment, taking the time to take stock of what I had seen. But the more I thought about it, the more the thoughts became blurred and jumbled in my mind.

Yellow eyes.

Inhuman speed.

Knife. Blood. Moonlight.

Tate.

When Mike finally moved toward the bed, he took my shoulders in his palms and stepped me back until my legs hit the edge of the mattress. I collapsed, slumping onto the bed as he guided me before he sat next to me. Once he started watching me, Mike didn't take his eyes off me, and I could feel his stare drilling into the side of my face while he waited for me to look at him, speak, or do anything at all.

"Tell me it wasn't real," I finally whispered. Because all I needed now was something to cling to. Everything had happened in a matter of minutes, and yet it felt like days ago that Mike and I had been fucking on the mattress we now sat on. I may have well been sitting next to a stranger.

"Tate is—"

"No," I cut him off, finally turning my head to meet his eyes, and I hated the pain I saw there because he didn't have the right to feel pain right now. I was the one who felt like my world was about to be turned upside down. "Not Tate." I frowned, gritting my teeth and trying to hold back the emotion. "You." Tentatively, I lifted my hand and cupped my palm over Mike's cheek. He was still a physical force to be reckoned with, but the way he tilted his head into my touch made him appear so small. I took my hand away. "Your eyes, I saw…"

What? What did I see?

"Yellow," I finished lamely. I looked up to see Mike watching me. His lips parted as if he were about to answer and then stopped. "Tell me it wasn't real, Mike, because Tate had the same eyes. Tell me he's a monster, you're real, and we're real together against this… force."

"I'm real," he whispered, choking back everything he wasn't saying. "But, I'm… not human."

Not human.

"I can't be here." I stood to leave, and Mike grabbed my wrist, moving to pull me back onto the bed, but I resisted. "Let me go."

"No."

"Mike, let me *go.*" I yanked against his grip, and he stood, towering over me and snatching my other wrist in his hand.

"You're not safe. You need to stay with me until Tate is no longer a danger."

"And whose fucking fault is *that?*" He flinched, and I didn't have it in me to feel bad. The images of our bodies moving together was now at the forefront of my mind, and here he was calmly telling me he wasn't... *human.* Mike was holding onto my hand and displayed no effort at all to contain my struggles. "What is Tate?" I demanded. "What are *you?*"

His eyes were haunted as he watched me, and inside somewhere, there was a twinge of sympathy. I knew this man, didn't I? At least, I thought I did. I wanted to save and protect him from whatever it was in his past that haunted him now. But this, *this* was too much.

"A demon."

I stopped struggling because, surely, he had to be joking. Although the words sounded like they caused him physical pain, the warmth of him burned against my wrists, and I let my gaze trail over his naked body. This can't be real—he looks too *human.* Part of me wanted to touch him, trace the lines of his hard chest, abs, and those incredible V-shaped muscles to tell myself he was human. I wanted to feel every divot of his pores, every scar, and every other imperfection. I needed to feel it all under my fingertips and then try to convince myself that this man couldn't possibly be a demon.

Because demons weren't real.

This can't be real.

CHAPTER 15

MIKE

It wasn't easy to convince Jacob that he needed to stay the night, and while I could have physically restrained him, I doubted that would help how he now felt toward me. I promised to sleep on the couch. Hell, I'd sleep on the fucking kitchen counter if he meant he would stay. I'd let him lock me in the closet and push a chair against the door if it meant he would try to get some sleep. I could hear him tossing and turning in the large bed, the silky sheets ruffling with every movement, and I wanted to ease his pain. But resisting going to him in the dark and brushing my fingers across his forehead and cheek was simply another test of my self-control.

If I had joined Frank's fight club and worked out my demon's needs, would my eyes have still changed in front of Jacob? Tate had set me on edge, and his simple presence was enough to make me feel younger and more inexperienced. I was right back to being the demon who first came to Earth with the hopes of living with the humans as one of them. A demon who was reminded with every step I *wasn't* human and never would be, and everything I touched turned to darkness because of a nature I couldn't escape. Tate craved the darkness, wanted it, and he was disappointed when his excitement over me being a demon was quashed by the reality I was nothing but a coward.

I marked him for life, and I don't blame him for hating me.

But I do blame him for coming after Jacob.

The confusion on Jacob's face when he saw my true eyes was haunting me—the delicate little frown that tarnished his features burned into my memory whenever I closed my eyes. For a moment, he forgot the blade at his throat and the danger he was in, the vulnerability of his nudity, and he was watching only me, knowing that I held some secret from him.

Now he knew and was scared and confused. Maybe it was better this way. If he grew to hate me because of what I was, then once Tate was dealt with, Jacob would leave and never come back. Then he wouldn't be corrupted by my demonic power, the part of me I couldn't escape.

Finally, Jacob fell into an uneasy sleep and

muttered and mumbled in his slumber. I thought I heard him say my name and an ache opened in my chest.

The pain was nothing less than I deserved.

Emrick was due back today, and Ilsa and Ray had come by my apartment in the afternoon to escort us to see him. It had been an awkward morning, and while Jacob had slept in, plagued by dreams that prevented him from sleeping during the remaining hours of the night, the rest of the time was spent in stony silence. He continually glanced at me as if expecting me to morph into a monster and attack him. I couldn't blame his reaction, but it still hurt for him to act as though I was keeping him captive when all I was trying to do was keep him safe.

I wouldn't leave Jacob alone for a second after what had happened. Somehow, Tate had escaped from Ray, and although she and Isla had searched, they hadn't found him and returned to my building. They avoided the cops milling around the entrance due to the doorman's murder and staked out the building for the remaining few hours of the night. But Tate did not attempt to return.

Frank said he would meet us at Urban, the nightclub Emrick ran his base from and where he also lived —evidently with his wife—although who would marry a fallen angel is beyond me.

Then again, who would bond with a demon?

There was no point in telling Frank he didn't need to be there. Now he had the confession about my past, he wasn't planning on letting me deal with any stage of this alone. He spent a decent twenty minutes this morning bellowing at me down the phone for not calling him last night after Tate had broken in, and I endured his rage, feeling my anger boiling in the pit of my stomach. Did he really think I *wanted* this shit to happen? But again, I didn't stop Frank's screaming nor stand up for myself because I would take every ounce of punishment I could get. I would accept every bit of pain and guilt, and let it pile on my shoulders and weigh me down because I deserved it all.

Eventually, Jacob stood and moved to the bathroom, not looking me in the eye, and showered and dressed with the door locked. When Ray and Ilsa came upstairs, he stuck close to Ilsa. Evidently, he could tell something was off about Ray from the looks he kept throwing her, and maybe he had his suspicions she was also a demon. I silently thanked Ilsa for not mentioning to Jacob she was bonded to Ray, and therefore, much like Tate, had elements of demonic power within her.

Jacob needed an ally somewhere.

When we arrived, Frank was leaning against his car, parked illegally in front of the club. Arms crossed over his impressive chest, he pushed himself upright and came to meet us, stopped in front of me, and didn't move until I met his eye. Without a word, he studied my face, reached out, and grabbed Jacob's arm as he walked past with his hands shoved in his pockets.

"Hey!" Jacob protested Frank's treatment, and I lifted my lip into a snarl.

"Get your hands off him."

Frank ignored me and stared into Jacob's eyes until Jacob's frown melted away from the intense glare, and his eyes grew wide with fear. "You're one of them, aren't you?" His voice trembled as he met Frank's gaze. Now that he had felt demonic power, he could sense it in the air around us, attuned to the aura that separated us from humans.

Frank scowled and released him before turning back to me. "I've been through all of this with Charlotte. He'll accept it one day."

I shook my head—this wasn't the same. Frank had willingly shown his nature to Charlotte after they had already built some semblance of a relationship. I glanced at Jacob over Frank's shoulder. He stood close to Ilsa as though I would attack him at any second. "I don't think so, Frank," I muttered, sidestepping and moving past him.

As a group, we moved to the club's entrance, the building ugly and imposing in the harsh sunlight. When the door creaked open, a man who resembled a bodybuilder stood, hand poised on the metal door, with colorful tattoos across his face, shaved head, and arms. He looked disinterested in our group until his eyes landed on Ray and Ilsa, and he scowled.

"What do you want?"

"We need to see Emrick," Ray said.

"I doubt he'll want to see *you.*"

"Fuck you, Sven. Just let us in."

Sven lifted a shoulder, opened the door wider, stepped aside, and let our odd group move through. Ray pushed her way to the front, and Ilsa brought up the rear, keeping her shoulder pressed close to Jacob's, which he didn't seem to mind. I was touched that she went out of her way to make him feel safe. When Ray treated this purely as the business transaction it was, Ilsa seemed to genuinely care about the man she was being paid to protect.

After being patted down by Sven, we made our way, single file, up a winding staircase, and Ray pounded on the door at the top of the stairs, immediately tapping her foot impatiently when it wasn't opened within two seconds of her demand for entrance. Another bodyguard opened the door, his tight black T-shirt two sizes too small and stretched across his arms, one side as heavily tattooed as Sven, though with less color. He, too, saw Ray and scowled but led her onto the balcony that overlooked the dance floor, and once everyone was inside, he left, closing the door with a metallic click behind him.

I barely had time to register footsteps pounding across the balcony before I was shoved to the side.

He was on Frank, his hand at Frank's throat, and had him shoved against the closed door. The guy was fucking huge and physically larger than Frank, which made him an imposing figure. Wearing black pants and a black tank, his arms and shoulders were covered in heavy tribal tattoos, his dark hair pulled back into a ponytail, the tip of which sat just above the hint of scars visible above the top of his tank.

The scars sent a shiver down my spine, the scars of a fallen angel whose wings had been removed.

Emrick.

A woman with chestnut hair was immediately at his back, grabbing his shoulders and attempting to pry him from Frank. "Emrick! What the fuck are you doing? What did he do?"

Her immediate reaction—*what did he do?* She didn't doubt that Emrick had a reason for attacking Frank. She studied Frank's smug face over Emrick's shoulder, and her expression changed, recognition dawning. "Oh, fuck."

Frank was grinning because that was his default look, but his eyes showed no recognition as he watched Emrick and the woman study him, and he seemed completely disinterested in Emrick's hand at his throat. When Ilsa moved in behind Emrick, she grabbed the back of the woman's dress and yanked her backward, sending her tumbling to the floor. Emrick turned with a roar of rage, and his momentary distraction gave Frank the upper hand, who spun him around and wrapped his forearm around Emrick's throat, pressing his back to his chest.

"Fucking let me go! Fucking *demon!*" Emrick spat. He was fighting against Frank's hold, but he was a fallen angel, and his strength, while still greater than a human, was no match for a demon of Frank's age.

"Calm the fuck down. I don't know your issue with me, but I'm pretty sure that's not what we're here for."

"I don't care what you're here for, I'm going to *fucking kill you.*" Emrick rounded on Ilsa. "And *you* for hurting Cara."

The woman pushed herself off the floor, throwing a dirty look at Ilsa. "She didn't hurt me, babe. I'm fine." Cara, this must be the wife, the kind of woman to marry a fallen angel and to stand by his side while he ran the largest underground crime syndicate in the city. She approached Emrick with a casual gait and touched his arm gently, ignoring Frank's stranglehold on her husband, and looked into his eyes or what she could see of Emrick's eyes behind the dark sunglasses he wore.

Emrick stopped struggling, and he and Cara stared at each other for a beat before Frank cleared his throat, asking the room in general, "Is someone going to tell me why this fucker attacked me?"

"You fucked her." Emrick pushed out through gritted teeth.

"What?" Frank was laughing now and increased his hold on Emrick when Emrick growled at him. "Who did I fuck?"

"My *wife,* you demon asshole!"

Frank frowned, studying Cara over Emrick's shoulder, no recognition on his face. My shoulders relaxed when Emrick stopped struggling against Frank. There was no need for me to intervene. Frank was more than strong and capable enough to take care of himself. I didn't realize just how much tension I was holding in my shoulders until I released it.

Emrick's jaw was tense as he clenched his teeth, but he kept looking forward, keeping his gaze, I assumed, on the woman he loved—Cara. She had a strange power over him, calming the beast but not quite taming him.

"When?" Frank asked, frowning, and I bit back the urge to chuckle. If he was going through a mental loop of all his sexual conquests before he found Charlotte, then we would be here for a while.

Cara shrugged. "It was years ago when I was a stripper at the Palace."

Frank laughed louder, and his amusement seemed to enrage Emrick anew. "Let me get this straight... I fucked your wife before you were married and even met?" He ventured, and Cara nodded slightly. "And because I'm a demon, you could smell me on her and recognized the scent." He was belly laughing now, his arm tightening around Emrick's throat with the movement and drawing a snarl from the fallen angel. "That's fucking gold, you overprotective son of a bitch. I'm not interested in her."

"You fucked her!" Emrick roared, his struggling beginning again, and I stepped forward, ready to intervene if necessary. Emrick was like a wild animal at this point, lashing out at Frank but unable to move him.

"I fuck *everyone!* I probably fucked your entire fucking club." Frank laughed, and I rolled my eyes as he winked at Cara before tilting his head back to speak into Emrick's ear. "Hell, I'm surprised I never fucked you. Now..." Frank snaked his other arm around Emrick's chest and crushed him against his own, "... are you going to behave if I let you go?"

Emrick moved, and from the way his feet lifted momentarily from the floor, it looked like he had attempted to launch himself backward onto Frank to unbalance him. It was evident he hadn't come up against a full-strength demon in a long while, and the remnants of celestial strength he relied on to intimidate and control humans weren't going to cut it when it came to Frank. Emrick seemed to decide fairly quickly that fighting was both a useless and humiliating endeavor and stopped struggling, nodding, and grunting. Frank straightened his arms, released Emrick, and shoved him away in one smooth motion. Emrick took it in his stride, collected Cara with an arm around her waist, and moved to the other side of the room. They mumbled to each other for a moment, Cara doing most of the talking, touching his cheek and stroking his arm before Emrick sat on the single chair by the rear balcony door, and Cara placed herself delicately on his lap.

Then, they simply watched us.

Ray cleared her throat, the first to break the tense silence that permeated the air. She opened her mouth to speak when I interrupted, tired of standing on the sidelines and letting everyone else sort this out. This had gotten out of hand already, and the fact that I stood there with a small entourage and not alone grated against me. Tate was my problem, my creation, and I needed to be the one who dealt with him.

"We're looking for Tate," I said, keeping my voice

steady despite the tremor of my hands.

"You're the severed partner," Emrick said. We stared at each other for a beat, and when I didn't answer, Emrick grunted. I didn't have the patience to tend to his sense of masculinity and whatever else he had going on that made him despise demons so much. "I don't know where he is."

"Obviously." I scowled. "But I need to know everything and anything you know that might help me find him."

"I can't help you."

"Can't or won't?"

"Take your pick."

I felt Jacob's eyes on me as Emrick unknowingly reflected my words back at me, but Jacob said nothing, and I couldn't bring myself to look at him right now.

"Do you want to kill him?" Emrick finally asked.

"No," I answered, and I swallowed against the temptation to continue talking because I didn't know enough about this Emrick to spill my secrets to him, and I suspected he felt the same about me. I didn't want to tell him I wasn't even sure the reasons I didn't want to kill Tate were purely because of the rules protecting demons or if because I felt I deserved to die more than he.

Emrick chuckled. "You may have no choice."

Again, he was sending my words back to me, and I hated the shiver it sent down my spine.

CHAPTER
16

JACOB

It felt like I was watching a play rather than something that was directly related to my life. It certainly didn't feel like the lines being played out were about someone who was a direct threat to Mike and me. The exchange between Frank and Emrick was bizarre. They were talking about demons like it was nothing, and as the conversation drew on, I took a few steps back, pulling myself into the shadows and away from the group in front of me.

Was I the only human in the room?

My heart was pounding against the inside of my chest, and I prayed they couldn't hear it, and I'm certain I was sweating. I wanted to run, to wrench the large door to my left open and simply bolt down the stairs and away. But what good would that do?

There was another demon, or human slash demon something, Tate, out for my life.

I wasn't safe anywhere.

Mike didn't want to return to his apartment, and I couldn't blame him. I didn't want to either but kept my mouth shut. Somehow, Mike negotiated with Emrick to let us stay the night in the club. Emrick was confident that not only would Tate not suspect we would be here, but even if he did, he wouldn't dare a direct attack. Emrick ran most of this city, apparently doing business I'd rather remain ignorant about, and the club was heavily guarded.

"One night," Emrick said, casting a glance at me like I was something unpleasant on the sole of his shoe before looking back at Mike. "One night only, then I'll call my brother, and your human can stay with him."

Mike's *human?* Is that what I had been reduced to? My nerves and fear were pushed to the side as a bubble of anger grew in my stomach.

"What if I don't want to stay with your brother?" I finally found my voice, and Emrick turned slowly to face me.

He sneered with little to no humor in the expression. "Don't worry... he's not like me. He's still a full-blown angel."

Wait! *What?*

I stuttered my way through the beginning of a million questions I never got to ask as Frank took his leave, shaking Mike's hand and lifting his other as if he were going to go in for a hug, then thought better of it. Ilsa and Ray left next, promising to continue searching for Tate and any information they could find.

"I think I know just who to ask," Ray said, opening the door and holding it askew for Ilsa.

"Earl?" Ilsa asked as she walked past, and Ray nodded, closing the door behind them.

I turned back to Mike and Emrick staring at each other with such intensity I doubted they were aware of anything going on outside of their bubble of mutual hatred. After a moment, Cara stood and held out an arm, inviting Mike and me through the door behind where she had been seated with Emrick as though we were formal guests. We walked through a large office, my legs trembling every step of the way, before entering a private elevator that took us up one floor to Emrick's apartment. The second we stepped across the threshold, I separated myself from the group. This entire setup was designed to keep me safe from Tate, but I didn't feel safe here with a demon, a fallen angel, and Cara, who was somehow totally okay with the knowledge of all of this. Perhaps I should pick her brain, but Emrick and Cara glanced at each other, and Cara licked her lips, drawing a growl from Emrick, who scooped her up. He tossed her over his shoulder and moved into the bedroom without another word, slamming the door behind him.

Mike turned to me but made no move to close the distance I had created between us. "Are you hungry?"

I shrugged. "I guess."

He nodded stiffly and moved to the kitchen, opening the refrigerator and searching the contents silently. I went over to a couch by a window and sat, curling my knees up to my chest and looking out at the city below. There wasn't much daylight left, and I listened to Mike moving around in the small kitchen and the increasing sounds from outside. People were starting to line up for the club already.

I wondered if they knew who the owner really was.

But I supposed they didn't care. Who would, right? I don't spend much time down this end of the city, but I know the corruption that exists here as well as everyone. The law is only effective unless someone is paying them out, and even Dad's friend, the mayor, isn't beyond reproach. I'm sure he could do something if he really set his mind and resources to it and clean up this city. But when his pockets are being lined as well as everyone else's, I can't imagine his motivation to take action would be particularly high.

I could live north of here and not have to think about these people and everything that happened in their day-to-day lives. I could sit at my desk and think only of the world that surrounds me within the walls of my cubicle, my thoughts occasionally escaping outside the office to a place where I have my own shop and can work with my hands, just me and my cars.

But now there was so much more to consider.

Was it morally wrong to start a sexual relationship with my father's main contractor? Perhaps.

Yesterday I thought that was the biggest moral quandary I would have to grapple with, but instead, I'm faced with a new question.

Is it morally wrong for a human to start a sexual relationship with a *demon?*

Demons and angels.

Fictitious.

Illusionary.

Completely unsubstantiated.

This seriously can't *be real.*

But the things I saw in Mike's place last night when he was facing off with Tate, the way Tate's touch made my skin crawl, and the scars... the *scars* they both shared, I realized now it was foolish of me to think they were anything normal. What could create scars like that? Matching scars that wound around both their arms and bodies as though bound together and torn apart.

Perhaps they were.

What do I know of demons?

I rubbed my temples, and my mind reeled.

Mike cleared his throat, and I looked up. He didn't quite meet my eyes as he handed me a plate with a couple of sandwiches, mumbling something about limited choices. When he sat on the opposite side of the couch, I scooted away from him slightly, realizing that my movement was anything but subtle with how his gaze found me, watching until I stilled. But he didn't quite meet my eyes, instead opting to focus on a spot around my collarbone. I remembered the feel of his mouth in that exact spot—hot and needy—and felt my cheeks flush. Mike cleared his throat again but said nothing. *Could he read my thoughts?* Fuck, I hope not.

We ate in silence, none of the awkwardness from this morning having dissipated throughout the day. If anything, it was worse now. I took a moment to study him, his thick lashes covering his eyes as he looked intently at his plate, every movement calculated. I felt that, like me, he wasn't really hungry but was eating more for something to do. He didn't seem to be enjoying his food as he had the steak we had together on our date, and I couldn't help but remember the cute humming sounds of approval he'd made on that night as he consumed the meal. I'm not even sure he was aware he was doing it, and he certainly didn't do it at the fancier restaurant.

There was a tug of sadness in my chest.

He was sweet.

He really was trying.

It was clearer now, the image of the man in front of me.

He was burdened with so much guilt from his past. Hell, who of us didn't have things we regretted? But I understood more now because he wasn't only holding himself responsible for his past, he was trying to pretend he was human. Constantly hiding beneath a mask and trying *so hard* to deny what he was. Every move he made was calculated, every word he said, and the business, suits, and car were all part of an image he created because that's who he wanted so desperately to be but knew he never would.

Did all demons feel this way? I thought about Frank, and he didn't seem to be suffering with the same burden of self that Mike was. *No, it can't be all demons then.* Ray also embraced her nature, throwing herself around and all but proclaiming *I am what I am.*

But Mike, he was troubled, constantly tortured by his nature.

"I'm sorry," he muttered.

My head snapped up, pulled from my thoughts. "What?"

Mike raised his head then, and the pain behind his gray eyes was like a punch in the gut, and I had to restrain the urge to slap my hand over my mouth to hide the trembling of my lip, feeling his pain with him.

And worst of all, I still wanted to help him.

He was the beast, lost and misunderstood like a goddamn fairy tale.

"I'm sorry about this… all of this. I never wanted you to be involved."

"Hell, Mike, when you talked about your crazy ex, I never imagined…" My lip twitched, almost a smile, and Mike caught the movement, and something that resembled hope flickered across his eyes before it was gone, replaced once again with guilt and self-loathing. I held his eye contact, and he let me, maybe sensing I needed this. The longer I looked into his gray eyes, so full of emotions and conflict, so human, it became harder to correlate the man in front of me with the beast I knew lay underneath.

I was sure I'd lose my mind before the end of the night.

"Can I see you?" I whispered.

Mike's hand shook as he took my empty plate and placed it with his on the ornate coffee table. "What do you mean?" He'd broken eye contact again, and I stared at him until he looked at me.

"I think you know what I mean. I want to see you, the *real* you."

Mike took my hands and stoked my palm with his thumb. "This is the real me," he muttered.

"The demon—"

"No," Mike interrupted me. His grip on my hands increased, and his words were punctuated by a growl. "The demon, that's not me. That's not who I ever wanted to be. I can't change what I am, but I can choose who I am. Don't take that away from me. Please."

I wanted to argue, but if even the idea of becoming the demon was physically painful for Mike—the sweat glistened on his forehead, and his grip on my hands caused my fingers to ache—I didn't want to be the cause of that for him.

"Do you hate me?" he asked.

"No." I shook my head, and it was the truth. How could I hate him? Because right now, I was battling with the idea that the most human and genuine man I had ever met was hiding a secret of this proportion. "I don't hate you."

Our conversation was broken when there was a shout from Emrick's bedroom. I jumped slightly at the deep "*Fuck!*" that rang out across the apartment, pressing my lips together to hide the smirk when it was quickly followed by a loud moan from Cara. When I turned back to Mike, he was almost smirking—almost. It pained me to see the confident businessman reduced to a nervous wreck in front of me. He was never afraid for his safety. He was afraid for me, scared, guilty, and hating who he was all at the same time.

I don't think he deserved all the hate he gave himself.

As if a test, Mike lifted his hand, pressed his palm to my cheek, and another growl pulsed through his throat when I leaned into his touch. I closed my eyes. "What are you doing?"

"Touching you," he whispered. His voice had darkened, and I wanted to open my eyes but was afraid I might see the yellow of his staring back at me, the man replaced with the monster.

"It feels different." I couldn't quite explain it, so I could only hope Mike would know what I meant. There were always sparks between us. Our bodies and minds moved in tandem when we were together in the bedroom, and his mouth and hands everywhere ignited passion in me on a level I'd never experienced before. But this was different. His hand was warmer, almost hot, and a current of electricity pulsed where he touched me, sending shockwaves of arousal straight to my cock, twitching in my pants.

When Mike didn't answer, I opened my eyes, relieved to see his gray ones staring back at me. "Demons, we need an outlet," he started, keeping his voice quiet and stroking his thumb across my cheek. "To keep in control of our human form. Usually fighting or fucking..." There was a flash of yellow across his eyes as he said *fucking,* and I sucked in a breath as my mind flooded with the image of his body above mine. "I had my own method of staying in control, but unfortunately, I recently lost access to that. Then with everything that happened with Tate, and you… *you…*" He traced his hand down until it was resting on my shoulder, and then he snaked his fingers around my throat, a growl rumbling through him as I swallowed against his fingers. "I desired you so much, to take you. What you're feeling now is my demon, pressing against me from the inside, desperate to take control. We're sexual beings. We radiate it, *ooze* it, and when we lose control, we can't help it."

"Feels good…" I whispered, swallowing again against his hand as he increased his grip on my neck.

"Yeah?" Mike was watching me. The dark expression was back, the one that promised power and pleasure and all things mind-blowing. There remained a hint of guilt hidden behind his eyes, but the more he touched me, the smaller it became until I could almost see the beast peeking out from behind his eyes, clawing to come out and play. I shuddered with the thought of being with Mike again, but I wasn't afraid, and the arousal was pins and needles across my skin and an explosion of sensations before he had even touched me.

I was reacting to his demon side, and it felt amazing. If he touched me more, I don't think I'd have the willpower to ask him to stop.

I didn't want him to stop.

Mike's expression darkened, and I bit my lip to hold back a moan as he moved his hand down, flicking my buttons undone one by one with expert fingers. When he shoved my shirt over my shoulders, he was no longer gentle, and the desperation of his movements was clear. I let him scoop an arm around my waist and lift me onto his lap, groaning when he bit and sucked at my neck. There was a voice in my head that screamed that this was wrong, and he was *literally* a monster, but I couldn't believe it. Because the Mike I knew would never hurt me and would only give me pleasure. My skin tingled everywhere he touched me, and I simply didn't have it in me to deny the lust he was creating.

"Mike, *fuck.*" His teeth sunk into my neck, not enough to draw blood but close, as his hands desperately clawed at my back. He growled again, ran a hand up the back of my head, tangling in my hair, and pulled my mouth to his. The second his tongue touched mine, I moaned. His taste was intoxicating, and was his tongue longer? At the realization, my mind simply became a blur of obscenities as Mike undid my pants and shoved his hand down the front, gripped my cock, and made me cry out.

His growl deepened before it became a snarl, and

he stood, taking me with him as I wrapped my legs around his body. I weighed nothing to him, and he didn't break his mouth from mine as he turned and dropped me back onto the couch, yanked down my pants, and exposed me to him.

"Get naked." I panted the words. "I want to feel your skin next to mine."

He was radiating so much heat I was surprised his clothes hadn't burst into flames because I sure as hell felt like I was about to. Leaning back slightly, he hesitated as his hands went to the buttons on his shirt, but systematically he undid them, and I tried not to stare as the scars on his chest were revealed. The gauze was gone, and the scars along his chest were an angrier red than those that covered the rest of his body. They must've been deep cuts, slicing back and forth across his chest. Were these new scars, or did he just not want me to see them last time? The question hovered on my tongue, but Mike swallowed it when he shrugged his shirt off and kissed me again.

Mike broke the kiss to run his tongue up my chest and over my nipple, making me jump. The sound of his belt and buckle clinking and being pulled undone filled my senses, and blindly, I groped forward, desperate to get my fingers around his cock. As he tugged his pants down, he shifted so I could wrap my fingers around his hard length, feeling the smoothness of his skin and running my thumb over the head of his cock.

Reaching between my legs, I stroked his length as he removed his shirt and let his pants fall to the floor. Grabbing my thighs, he tilted my hips back and plunged his tongue between my cheeks.

"Oh *fuck!*"

Mike pressed his tongue against my hole, coaxing me to open up to him. His grip on my thighs was almost painful as he bent me back at the hips, exposing me fully to him and working his tongue in and around my ass. He expertly prepared me to be fucked, and although I knew the man between my legs was no man, not human, I still ached for his touch, for him, and I couldn't concentrate on anything but the feel of his hands and tongue. When he slid a finger inside me, I saw stars and failed to contain the volume of my moan when he added a second. Mike gripped my cock, working my length in tandem with his fingers inside me, and I gripped the couch, a mixture of incomprehensible words and sounds falling from my lips.

"Fuck me, please," I begged him. I watched his eyes as the yellow passed over them again, lingering as he stared at me, the possessiveness evident in his gaze and sending a hot flush over my body.

Spitting on his hand, Mike worked it around his cock and positioned himself between my legs, the head of his cock pressing against my entrance. The almost constant rumbling growl in his chest continued, and where he gripped the couch next to my head, the fabric tore and gave way as he pushed forward, stretching me to my limit. Achingly slowly, he pushed in, and my hands shot to his forearms, gripping him as my mouth hung open, taking in the delicious stretch of him.

Rocking his hips against mine, he took his time, pushing in a little deeper with each thrust. Mike's breathing was heavy and ragged. I studied his face and the twitch of his jaw as he clenched his teeth together.

He was holding back.

"Mike," I whispered, and when he opened his eyes, they were still yellow, a frown deepening on his forehead before they cleared to gray. "It's okay, you don't need to hold back."

"Don't want..." The words were jagged as he pushed them through his clenched teeth. "Don't want to hurt you."

"You won't." I can't even say how I knew that, but I felt it in every fiber of my being. He wouldn't hurt me. He never would.

There was a brief moment of lingering hesitation before he snapped his hips forward, pressed flush against my ass, and completely penetrated me. I cried out, gripped his back, and Mike waited a beat for a protest that wouldn't come before he began fucking me with hard, relentless thrusts. Every movement almost drove me over the edge as the head of his cock rubbed against that sensitive part inside me that exploded with pleasure.

He was animal, snarling and growling, grabbing at my shoulders and the couch cushions, driving into me, forcing me to spread my legs and tilt my hips up to give him access to all of me. This is what it was like to be completely taken, to be held, protected, and *owned*. This is where Mike met the demon in the middle, and together they shared the power of the man on top of me, making me shudder and tremble under his touch and thrusts.

My peak was building, every hit of his cock against my prostate pushed me closer until I was whimpering in Mike's ear, the sound merging perfectly with the growl moving through his throat.

"Mike," I panted out, my fingers aching from where they gripped his shoulder blades. "I'm going to…"

"You're *mine*," Mike snarled, hitting me with another hard thrust in exactly the right spot.

"Yes," I hissed out through my teeth.

"*Mine!*" This time the word was punctuated with a long and harsh growl, and I spasmed around him as I came, cum shooting over my stomach. Mike's arms trembled, and the fabric ripping on the couch cushions intensified as he unloaded inside me, twitching and thrusting his cum into me.

He collapsed on top of me, and the gentle ache of

his cock, still hard , was so good.

There was a moment filled with nothing but our breathing, his heartbeat against mine as we came down from our highs.

"Do I scare you?" Mike whispered against my neck.

It was strange, but there was something about discovering Mike's secret that changed everything, but not in the way I would have thought it would. Of course, I had been afraid initially, but was I still? Or was the man and beast now merged into one—one man who would protect me, look after me, claim me—a warrior.

And beyond that, a man who trusted me with every part of him, even the parts he hated and the parts he couldn't control.

"No," I answered, planting a kiss against his collarbone.

Mike simply hummed in return, a sound filled with satisfaction and only hinted at uncertainty. We lay there for some time, with Mike buried inside me, and every twitch of his cock would send another bolt of pleasure through me.

"I'll protect you…" he said, and it almost sounded like he was talking to himself, reassuring himself more than he was me, "… always. I'll keep you safe. Whether you hate me or not or whether you stay with me or not, I'll protect you."

I believed him.

CHAPTER
17

JACOB

Mike's arms were wrapped around my shoulders, keeping my back firmly against his chest as he slouched slightly to keep his face near mine. I didn't want him to let me go, and in a room with angels and demons, I tried not to think too hard about the irony it was that with the demon, I felt the most secure.

Demon or not, he was Mike.

Ray and Ilsa hadn't returned, and despite Frank calling this morning, Mike had insisted we were okay, and he didn't need to be here for the handover.

Handover, like I was illegal goods or something.

Zaqiel, Emrick's brother, was in Emrick's words a *full-blown angel*, had come to pick me up. I trusted Zaqiel almost immediately, and while he was a tall and imposing figure like his brother, he radiated calm and security. He had deep blue eyes that watched me, expressionless, and Emrick and Mike ran through who was after me and why. Mike did most of the talking while Emrick remained tight-lipped about his experiences with Tate. I was to stay with Zaqiel and his human partner—Evie—for a few days or as long as needed until Tate could be brought under control.

In Mike's world, that meant reasoning with Tate somehow, but for Emrick, it meant to kill him. I didn't know what Emrick's stakes in this were, but it was almost like he'd been handed a pass that said *go,* and now he could kill Tate and use Mike and me as an excuse for his deeds. Is that how he played his entire business? Waiting until he had some flimsy excuse to kill that he could cling onto so he didn't need to feel remorse?

I wanted to stay with Mike, but Mike and Tate shared a connection. Mike had explained to me what bonding meant between demons or between a demon and a human and what it meant to sever the bond, an act that had left him and Tate scarred for life, inside and out. Tate would be able to find Mike if we stayed together, and Mike feared that he would somehow subconsciously call to him in moments of passion. Emrick was steadfast that Tate wouldn't come to the club, but Mike was taking no chances with my life.

So, an angel was to be my babysitter.

I kept glancing over Zaqiel's shoulders as though I would see a glimpse of feathered wings, and that would somehow make this all real. There was a lingering part of my mind telling me I was going crazy, that none of this was real, and that Emrick, Mike, Zaqiel, and Tate were all merely deluded humans.

Zaqiel's partner, Evie, sauntered up behind him, watching Emrick with distaste and distrust, which made me like her immediately. She was stunning, the epiphany of traditional beauty, except for the scars. Not scars born from a severed bonding like Mike's. No, these were from another person. Her scars told the tale of abuse. Yet when she saw me looking, and I raised my eyes to her, ready to apologize, she simply smiled softly, reassuring me it was okay. She was comfortable with every part of her, and I envied that.

It may have been platonic, but I think I fell in love with Evie right there, and I can see how an angel would love her too.

Emrick stood and took several large steps across the balcony floor to Zaqiel, where they briefly but strongly shook hands. A slap of palms together and a single shake was all before Emrick dropped the contact. Zaqiel seemed unfazed by Emrick's behavior, but I suppose, as his brother, he was probably used to it.

Emrick turned to Evie and looked her up and down. "Weren't you a hooker?" he asked.

I almost choked on my breath, and Evie casually arched an eyebrow at him. "Excuse me?"

Emrick waved his hand up and down near her body. "You're a bit fatter."

Zaqiel opened his mouth to protest, a deep frown etched between his perfect brows. Before he could even get a word out, Evie had balled her hand into a fist and landed a punch on Emrick's nose. Emrick's head snapped back, but otherwise, he didn't move, slowly lowering his head to glare at her. Evie appeared delicate next to the towering structures that were the angel and ex-angel brothers, but she hadn't slapped him, not a Hollywood-esque slap across the face. She'd punched him with enough force I'm sure a human would have been knocked on their ass.

Quietly, I was impressed, and inwardly I chuckled, but judging by the darkness creeping onto Emrick's expression, I decided to keep my mouth shut.

"I'm pregnant, you fucking asshole!" she snapped.

"Congratulations," I muttered. It was an automatic response, although that didn't make it any less genuine. I almost chuckled again at the way Evie's expression changed in an instant from fury to a smile when she turned to me and then to anger when she looked back at Emrick. Zaqiel placed a hand on Evie's arm and pulled her behind him, glaring at Emrick while Evie muttered something about *men with power* and someone called *Tyson.*

Zaqiel turned to me and held his hand out. I had to maneuver my arm to get to him, Mike repositioning his arms around me, holding me tight even while I shook Zaqiel's hand.

"Zaqiel," he said, his voice deep and soothing. "It's nice to meet you, although I regret it's under these circumstances."

"Jacob. Thank you for your help."

It all felt incredibly formal, and this wasn't my element. I was out of place, albeit for different reasons. I was as much of an outsider here as I was in the office surrounded by business-minded people who weren't like me, wishing they were working outside and getting their hands dirty.

"Come, we'll head straight back to mine."

Zaqiel hadn't let go of my hand, and when Mike didn't loosen his grip on me, Zaqiel pulled me forward. There wasn't much strength behind the tug, but enough to get his message across—*it was time to go.*

I didn't want to leave Mike. The revelation about his true nature and the beings we were dealing with had thrown me. But *last night* had been something else. How could I feel safe in his arms, knowing he was a demon? But I absolutely did, somehow more than ever. He was a constant, my rock in this world that I no longer understood, a bridge between my world and his, where he felt more alive and human than most people I'd met. They drudged through the day-to-day, but Mike lit up everything inside me, and I wanted to cling to that and the security he offered for as long as I could.

Slowly, Mike's arms unraveled from around me, and the air was a stinging cold against me without his warmth. Zaqiel let go of my hand as I came level with him, and he nodded at me before I turned to face Mike. The space between us might as well have been miles for the way he watched me.

Zaqiel turned to Emrick. "This Tate, isn't he one of yours? Why don't you bring him into line as you do?"

"He never was one of mine."

I used the time that Zaqiel and Emrick stared at each other to watch Mike. I wanted to memorize every line of his face. His five o'clock shadow was stronger now, bordering on becoming a beard as he hadn't shaved in days, with flecks of gray throughout to match his hair. His jaw was tense and moving as he ground his teeth, and like mine, his hands twitched, wanting to reach out but resisting the urge.

"Let's go." Evie reached out and took my hand, and reluctantly I turned, craning my neck to watch Mike as long as I could.

"I'll come get you as soon as I can." Mike's voice may have been steady, but in his eyes, I could see the hurt and the break of him.

"I'll be waiting," I whispered.

CHAPTER
18

MIKE

Left alone with Emrick, we stood in stony silence for too long. Neither of us wanted to be the one to break it, but the longer we stood there, the more time we wasted, and we should be searching for Tate.

But where to start?

Emrick had made it clear that if Tate didn't want to be found, he wouldn't be, and since he already had a price on Tate's head that had come up with nothing, our chances of locating him now were slim.

But evidently, Tate had a weakness.

Me.

Somehow, I needed to lure him to me now that Jacob was safe and out of the way of the tornado of danger that Tate posed. If I could get him alone, even if I had to tie him to a damn chair, maybe we could have an actual conversation.

Failing that, I'd leave him to Emrick.

Most of the guilt I had been battling with about taking Tate's life had ebbed away the moment he had placed a knife against Jacob's throat. If he had no qualms about taking away someone who mattered to me or ending an innocent life, then why should I care about leaving him with a fallen angel who would almost definitely kill him?

Because that wasn't me, that was the demon speaking.

The demon who was controlling more and more with every hour that passed.

Finally sick of the silence, I turned to Emrick to start formulating a plan when the balcony door behind me shuddered. A sickly *bang* echoed out again as someone was thrown against the door from the other side a second time, the recognizable sound of an unconscious body slumping to the floor followed. Emrick reached behind him, pulled out a revolver, and checked the bullets before pointing it directly at me.

"Get out of the way, you fucking idiot," he said, pushing the words through gritted teeth. I scowled at him and stepped to the side, giving him a clear shot of the door as it burst open, and a young man with messy dark hair stormed into the room. He was rage and fire and radiated enough power for me to know this wasn't a lightweight, although he wasn't as old as me.

Beyond his anger, his nature was clear as day. Another demon.

"Where is she, you *fuck?*" He raged, directing his anger at Emrick who rolled his eyes, ignoring the way the younger demon was shaking, his hands balled into fists at his sides. Emrick slid the gun back into his pants and crossed his arms over his chest. It took me a moment, but beyond his twisted expression, I recognized this demon. He was Frank's younger brother, Cade, and I had no idea he was living on Earth. Sibling relationships weren't strong amongst demons, and if you put a dozen demons who were related together, they were more than likely to tear each other apart than a dozen strangers who would fuck each other.

Demons had two modes—fuck or fight—and if they couldn't do one, they'd resort to the other.

Cade stormed across the balcony, stopping when Emrick held a hand between them. Although Cade's shoulders were heaving with every aching breath he took, he simply glared at Emrick and waited for him to speak.

"What are you talking about?" Emrick sounded almost bored, and this only seemed to enrage Cade more.

"Nikki! She's fucking *gone*, and I found your fucking product in her car."

Emrick barked out a laugh, and Cade's lip

twisted. "Maybe she likes the snow," he said, chuckling.

Cade roared an indistinguishable sound not made up of any words. "She was *clean.* She's always been *clean.* You must've dropped some of your shit when you took her."

Emrick threw his hands up. "You're a fucking idiot. I thought maybe you would have grown a bit in the years since I've seen you, but apparently, you're still as naïve now as you were then." He lifted a hand again when Cade went to interrupt. "*Why,* dear Cade, would I leave some of my product behind if I were going to kidnap someone? *Why* would I leave behind something that led straight back to me?"

"Then who took her?"

"What makes you think I know anything?"

Cade closed the space between them, pressing his finger against Emrick's chest. "You're involved. I know you are. You're always involved in this shit. Everything that goes down in this city has your grubby fingerprints all over it. She's a fucking cop, Emrick. You won't get away with this."

"I'd say I've done nothing, but it's a lie. But this is the truth, I had *nothing* to do with *this.*"

"Who's Nikki?" I spoke up, sick of being on the outside of Emrick's bullshit interactions, who seemed to somehow be in a fight with everyone he came across. First Ray, then Evie, and now Cade.

The guy certainly hasn't made himself many allies.

"My…" Cade seemed to be searching for the right word, and Emrick chuckled when Cade finally settled on 'partner.'

"Oooh," Emrick goaded. "Didn't she ever bond with you? That's too sad. Mike here has bonded before, and he's already started a new one."

"Shut the fuck up, Emrick." I hissed, only enticing another laugh. *Fuck, I hated him.*

Emrick casually rubbed his chin, able to ignore the burning rage from the demon in front of him. "You know, Cade, you might benefit from looking for Tate."

"Tate? Who the fuck is Tate?"

"Do you remember all those years ago when you first came to see me? When you were convinced I was involved in Nikki's drama? Do you remember how you two just *strolled* right on into my club and up here to see me without question?"

"What are you getting at?" Cade barked. "Spit it out."

"Tate saw Nikki, and he told me to let her up here to see me." Cade's eyes widened, but he said nothing as Emrick continued, "If anyone has her, it may be him."

"What's the connection between them?" Cade asked.

Emrick lifted a shoulder. "Don't ask me. But there are always those around who tend to know these things."

Cade roared again, "Fucking *Earl*," and he punched the wall next to the balcony door, cracking the plaster and drawing a snarl from Emrick. "I'll kill that son of a bitch."

Before I could ask anything further of the demon, he ran down the stairs, his feet pounding on the metal as it creaked under his weight.

I turned to Emrick. "What the fuck was that all about?"

His lip twitched. "An old friend."

"Oh yeah? He didn't seem that fucking friendly with you."

Emrick dropped into his seat. "What do you want from me, Mike? One doesn't make many friends in my business."

"What if he finds Tate? Why didn't you ask him to stay so we can work together?"

Emrick shrugged. "We don't need him."

"You're an asshole."

"I know. Now…" he held up a finger, and I gritted my teeth as I cut off my protest, "… we need to figure out what *we're* going to do about our mutual friend now that your boyfriend is safe with my dear brother—"

Credit to Emrick that when the balcony door flew open the second time, he was on his feet once again with his gun pointed faster than I had registered what was happening. I recognized Ilsa and Ray at the same second Emrick did, but he didn't lower his gun, instead shouting, "Doesn't anybody have any fucking respect anymore? This is my fucking *business.*"

Ray simply arched an eyebrow at him. "Are you going to lower the gun?" Emrick did, a vein twitching in his neck and his jaw clenched tight while Ray regarded him. "You know your bouncers are unconscious, right?"

"All of them?"

"All of them. Someone flew in here like a fucking tornado. I'm impressed."

Emrick scowled. "Just an old friend."

Ilsa scoffed out a quiet laugh. "Yeah, right."

"Enough! I'm not here for your goddamn drama. What did you find out?"

Ray looked ready to argue with me at my outburst, flicking her long hair over her shoulder before Ilsa held her arm out and threw her a significant look that I can only assume meant *rein yourself in.* "We finally found Earl, and he looked much too pleased with himself."

"Earl?" I asked. This was the second time he had been mentioned in as many minutes. The name sounded vaguely familiar, but where I had heard it before, I couldn't remember.

"Demon, old, very old. Powerful and corrupt as hell. He'll do anything for money." Ray cast a glance at Emrick. "I believe he worked for you at some point."

Emrick shrugged. "I've hired him once or twice."

Ray rolled her eyes. "You have no standards at all, do you?"

"Careful, I seem to remember hiring you as well."

Ray pouted and made another scoffing sound but said nothing further. After a beat with my heart drumming in my chest and images of Tate hovering behind my eyes, I finally snapped. Was I the only one here with a sense of urgency? I wanted this over and done with so I could go back to my life and finally stop being chased by my past.

Maybe there was a future with Jacob if he still felt the same even after the adrenaline from all this was gone.

"And?" I exploded, throwing my arms up. "What did you find out?"

"He knows something, but he'll only speak to you." Ilsa gave me a significant look, and I had no idea how to translate it.

"He doesn't even know me."

"Evidently, he knows *of* you."

"I don't like it," Ray chimed in. "It sounds like a setup. I wanted to cut him until he gave us answers, but the guy gives me the creeps."

I moved toward the door. There was no question. Last night Jacob had submitted to me, and afterward, we had connected on another level. Every second I spent with him was forging a connection that was something beyond a demon bonding, something that I couldn't touch or see. He was under my skin, inside my head, and in every beat of my heart. I wanted him every day for the rest of mine, and right now, every step I took was about keeping him safe. "I have to go."

Emrick stood. "I'm coming too."

"You don't seem a team-player type."

"I don't like games, and he's fucking with me. I'm going to kill that asshole." I have no idea if he meant Earl or Tate, and I didn't ask. Then he added, "I'm just as invested as you."

"I highly doubt that."

As we moved toward the door, Emrick reached behind him, patting over his pants as if to reassure himself of the weapon he held. I felt exposed without anything and hadn't even considered arming myself. It felt wrong to do so. Going to find Tate armed was pre-empting a step I didn't want to take. I turned to Ray and Ilsa, who were my protection. "You coming?"

They didn't answer straightaway and looked at each other before Ray said, "We might have other leads we can follow up on."

"I think it might be best if you stick with us. We might need your skills."

"And muscles." Ray flexed her arms.

"This isn't a goddamn joke, Ray," I hissed at her. "If you come and protect me, I'll pay you double."

There was another shared look between them, and Ilsa whispered, "We could do a lot of good with that money."

"Fine, let's go." Ray held the door open and stepped over the bouncer, who was beginning to stir. Emrick grunted and kneeled next to him, slapping him lightly on the face. A few muttered words were exchanged, and Emrick helped him to his feet and down the stairs, seating him in a booth around the corner. He checked on every one of his men on the way to the front door, making sure they were all okay after Cade's attack. It seemed an oddly compassionate move for someone with a reputation for being nothing but brutal.

Before we left, he explained to Cara where he was going. She'd been working the floor, and didn't like the sound of our plan. Rage exploded from her. "I'm coming with you."

"The fuck you are." Emrick's rage mirrored hers, and they stared at each other, anger swirling around in their eyes, hardly a lover's embrace.

"I want to kill him after what he did to you."

Emrick chuckled and placed a hand on Cara's shoulder, wrapped his other hand around her neck, pulled her against him, and slid his tongue into her mouth. "Fuck, I love you, pussycat. But you need to stay here and run the business. I'll kill him for both of us... that's a promise."

She glared at him, licking her lips slowly before

nodding. They exchanged another overly passionate kiss, not at all bothered, it seemed, by the fact they had an audience, their hands trailing across each other before we left.

We had barely made it a handful of steps toward the alley that ran down the side of the club to get to Emrick's van before we were ambushed.

CHAPTER 19

MIKE

Zaqiel swooped in, glancing behind him as he landed and folded his wings away as if a slight glance behind him would tell him if anyone had witnessed his wings on the way.

He was alone, and immediately the panic jumped my heartbeat up another notch, the pounding echoing in my ears, and I tried desperately to contain the mixture of emotions that rose in my chest.

"Where's Jacob?"

"Mike, I'm sorry—"

"Sorry? What are you sorry about? What the fuck happened?" My panic jumped another notch, and beyond that was the clawing on the inside of my skin, my demon desperate to get out and get to Jacob. We'd started a bond, and on an instinctual level, I felt I owned him now. That instinct was mixing with my particularly human emotions, creating a turmoil of conflict that built and crashed over itself over and over again like a tidal wave of panic, rage, and fear.

"He was taken by a demon—"

"Tate?"

"No, a demon. Very old, ancient, incredibly powerful. I barely kept Evie safe—"

"Evie? What the fuck about Jacob?"

"I tried."

"He was with you for all five fucking seconds, and you let him get taken?" My fingers stretched and clamped, bending at the knuckles and where there were no joints in humans as my demon came closer to the surface. Right now, Zaqiel was the enemy, and his eyes flared a bright white as I closed the gap between us in two brisk strides and shoved hard at his shoulders. Zaqiel took a step backward to counteract my attack but moved no more. Picking a fight with an angel was beyond a bad idea, but emotions were swirling around inside me, and a surge of desire for violence was an extremely real reminder that beyond letting go a bit too much last night, I hadn't satiated my demon as much as I should.

I'd been on Earth for a long time. I should know better than to think I could control it through willpower alone.

Zaqiel's hand found my throat, his arm outstretched, keeping as much space between us as possible as I took a swing at him. When he spoke, his voice was deep and ethereal, a mixture of tones and sounds that made it clear he was holding back his own power. "Don't make the mistake you're the only one who cares," he grumbled, his fingers tightening on my throat. "I did all I could." He let me go with a shove that had me reeling for a few steps to right myself. I went to move forward again, and a hand landed on my shoulder. Turning to Ray, she didn't even flinch at the rage in my eyes and simply shook her head.

"Let's go get that creep," she said.

Roaring in frustration, I turned and sprinted toward Emrick's van.

Emrick and the women followed, muttering obscenities.

"I'm going to get Evie somewhere safe, and then I'll keep looking," Zaqiel called at our retreating backs.

But he'd failed me once, and I no longer trusted him with Jacob's safety and life.

If the angel couldn't save him, then the demon would.

Earl lived in a rundown townhouse and opened the door slowly, casually, as though there wasn't a group of beings on his doorstep after his head. The top of his shaved scalp scraped the doorway as he moved forward to assess us, his arms too long for his body draped lazily down his sides, and one hand sat purposefully on the doorknob.

"May I help you?" Earl drawled.

I'd had enough, everything was unraveling around me, and the part of me that wanted to maintain my humanity was dripping away steadily. Slowly, I was returning to who I was, my demon in control and seeking only vengeance. Shoving Earl in his chest, he stumbled backward, his look of indifference morphing into one of rage before settling into amusement.

"You're older than you appear," he muttered, smirking.

"Where is he?" I demanded.

Earl gazed over my shoulder as Ilsa closed the door behind her, the sound of Emrick checking the bullets in his gun drawing Earl's attention. Emrick was no fool. Bullets wouldn't kill this demon, but at least if they were silver, they would inflict a hell of a lot of pain if the shot sites were chosen carefully—perhaps in the back of the neck or through the shoulder or jaw.

"Emrick, so good to see you again. Have you come to rehire me?" His voice remained calm, a deep monotone as though this were any other day. But he didn't bother hiding the dual tones created when demonic power seeped through the vocal cords, almost sounding like static.

"Fuck off, Earl. Where is Tate?"

"I was meant to tell you where he was." Earl's gaze dragged back to mine, every movement he made was slow and purposeful, and a muscle in my jaw twitched. My instinct was to attack him, but a part of me whispered inside my head—*run.*

"So, tell me," I said.

"I was meant to tell you, not your entire entourage." He sighed heavily, dropping his shoulders. "But Tate didn't say I wasn't supposed to betray him after I helped him with his tasks, so I don't really care."

"Why are you doing this?" Ray asked.

His gaze moved to her, the same slow movement through the hall, stopping and lingering on each of us in turn. "I'm loyal to no one."

"Where. Is. He?" I pushed the words through gritted teeth.

"You asked that question very much like Cade did."

"Cade? What did you do to him?" If I had to tell Frank something had happened to his baby brother…

"Nothing." Earl scowled. "He got the upper hand on me and took a knife to my chest. I told him what he wanted to know before he destroyed my mark."

"Holy shit." Emrick sounded impressed. "He's a bold son of a bitch. I should've hired him years ago."

Earl's eyes narrowed at Emrick, then he turned back to me. "I did what Tate asked. I took the girl, then he needed help, so I took the boy as well."

"What girl?" Ilsa asked, panic edging her voice, unsuccessfully hidden behind her tone.

"That would be Nikki, Cade's partner." I turned back to Earl. "For fuck's sake, get to the point. Where is Tate, and what has he done with Jacob?"

"As far as I know, he hasn't done anything with the boy…" when he smiled, my skin crawled, "…yet. I believe that's a show he's waiting for you to witness."

"Where the fuck is he?" If I had to unleash my demon, I would, and to hell with the consequences.

Earl ran his tongue around the inside of his lips. "Darkside."

Emrick hissed an animal sound that had the hairs on the back of my neck standing up. He was beyond a fallen angel now, he was pure darkness. The sounds he made to express his anger and discontent were more animal, more demon than angel. Hearing those sounds from an angel, fallen or otherwise, was disturbing.

"You're kidding," he spat the words out.

Earl smiled, a lopsided grin exposing sharp, yellowing teeth, more on one side of his mouth than the other. "Amusing, yes?"

"No," Emrick said, and at my raised eyebrow, he explained. "Darkside was one of my clubs. It was burned down, and there's nothing but a shell left."

Earl clicked his tongue against the inside of his cheek, clearly enjoying the exchange and intensity flowing through the air between the group. "I'd love to stick around for the fun, but this town has become messy. I have connections elsewhere, so I need to start making plans to move."

"Where are you going to go?" Ilsa asked, her tone filled with suspicion instead of curiosity.

"Like I'd tell *you.*"

"Come on," I said, waving my hand before lowering it quickly as the black spots had begun to appear across my skin. The idea that Jacob was so close but in such danger was surging through my blood, and with every step I took, my demon screamed and clawed to get out and take control of the situation.

But I knew what that would look like—all blood, violence, and no thought—and I couldn't risk Jacob getting caught in the crossfire.

Or seeing me for what I truly am.

As we turned to leave, Emrick asked Earl, "Why did you leave my product when you took the girl? Why try to frame me? I can't imagine what you have to gain from that."

Earl shrugged, his lips curling again into an unsettling smile. "It was funny, no?"

Emrick snarled at him. "Get the fuck out of my city." And we left with the sound of Earl's dark chuckling following us out the door.

CHAPTER
20

TATE

A literal cage, they appeared to be designed to house some sort of large animal but were instead for the dancers who used to occupy this bar. Once upon a time, it was a simple pub, but there's more money to be made when there are half-naked women dancing, so Emrick had the cages installed, lockable, to keep the dancers safe from the drunken shenanigans of the patrons. It was amusing as hell to see Nikki, my dear sister, in there, gripping the bars and staring at me with an expression crossed between anger, disbelief, and fear.

It was the last part that was my favorite, and I looked forward to making it worse.

Her white-blonde hair, the same shade as mine, fell over her shoulders, and despair crept into her mind the longer she was there. She would occasionally open her mouth like she was going to say something, then close it, and simply continue to watch me.

Slumping down against the wall opposite the cage, I watched her, balancing the knife's handle on my knee and turning it, ignoring the small drop of blood that formed against my fingertip as it spun.

"If you have something to say, just say it."

Nikki watched me for a beat longer. "Why are you doing this?"

"Everything that was meant to be mine, Dad took away because of you, and I've spent the better part of a decade fighting to get it ready to take back."

"I didn't have any say in what Dad did. I didn't even know who he really was until after he died."

Standing abruptly, I dropped the blade, snickering at how Nikki backed against the other side of the cage as I approached. I lifted my gun out of the back of my pants, twirling it around so it caught the light against the few parts that weren't covered in grime. "Do you recognize this?" Nikki shook her head, and I tutted. "It's the only thing Dad ever gave to me. How sweet it would be to use it to kill the daughter he loved as much as he hated me."

"Why? Why now?"

"Two of my worlds have collided, and the opportunity to make the most of it and bring you both together was too delicious to pass up."

Nikki cast a sideways glance at the man in the

cage next to her, his thick blond hair covered his face, his cheek pressed against the cement. Unconscious. "Who is he?"

"He's my ex's new squeeze."

"Thomas, *please.*" She cautiously approached the cage wall closest to me as though she were advancing on a wild animal.

"Don't call me by that name," I snarled out. Thomas was gone. Thomas was the man who thought he would inherit his father's business, the man who thought his father was strong enough not to get taken by the charms of an Aryan beauty, the woman who brought Nikki into our lives.

"Please," she whispered, her hands once again wrapping around the bars, delicate fingers against the cold steel that kept her captive. "Don't do this. I never hated you."

"But *I* hated *you.* I hated everything about you. I wanted to *sell* you. You and your pretty white-blonde hair would fetch a high price with Dad's clients."

She recoiled at my words. "I'm your sister. We're family!"

"You were never part of our family. You were sheltered from the truth, from the abuse that came with it, from the things I had to witness and take part in. I became exactly what Dad made me, and then he kicked me out. Exactly like Mike. I'm the creation of other men, of demons, and then when they don't like what they've created, they blame me." Scoffing to myself, I ran a finger over the gun in my hands. I needed to center myself because I was getting off track. Talking to Nikki like this would do nothing except give her false hope that she could somehow reason with me.

Turning on my heel, I stormed away from Nikki's cage. I no longer wanted to look at her because I don't think I could stare at her this entire time while I waited for Mike to come to me. It wouldn't take long for him to get the information from Earl, not with Ray and Ilsa by his side. Pretty much any shit goes down in the city that is outside of Emrick's reach, and you can assume Earl is involved somehow.

When Mike came, I would kill Nikki first. He didn't know her, but he didn't need to. She was an innocent, and that would be enough to torture him, along with the satisfaction I would get from doing to her exactly what our father did to me, and much worse. Then I'd turn on his fuck toy and make him scream in pain before taking his life.

Only when Mike was broken would I kill him too.

Turning, the scent of a demon made my nostrils twitch. But this wasn't Mike. The scent was familiar, and I tried to place it.

"Cade!" Nikki cried out, and I spun on the spot. He was barreling toward me, all yellow eyes and fury. Bordering on losing control of his demon, his skin dappled with pops of black and glowing red. I only had moments to reflect on the irony that my sister and I had chosen demons as partners before he was on me.

I'd smelled him in her home on previous days when I'd been there to scout out the location, and I figured there was a chance he would come for her. My only regret was I hadn't finished rigging the cages up yet, but that would come soon. Cade could be controlled via Nikki, and that was all I needed to know.

And discovering her partner was a demon opened up an interesting opportunity to control his strength. As he bowled me over, I reached down, scooped up the knife I had abandoned only minutes earlier, and drove it into his chest. Cade roared, tossing his head back, his mid-length dark hair falling back from his face. Without letting go of the handle, I dragged the blade down before removing it. It wasn't as deep as I had hoped. He was fast, but young, and I was able to get at least an inch into his flesh. The blade was silver, but that didn't account for the severity of his reaction, and it was only when the fabric of his T-shirt flapped open to reveal his chest that I understood.

He'd had his pentagram removed, the mark that allowed demons to move between Hell and Earth. I recognized the shape of the scars because I'd seen Mike's mark glow when our bond was being severed, and he was barely in control of the pain.

Cade reared back, his first instinct to protect his chest, and I took the brief opportunity to slash at him again, hitting everywhere I could get—his arms, torso, legs, and then his back, every inch of his skin he made the mistake of exposing to me. He was fighting in a flurry with nothing practiced or thought through about his movements, and I forced myself to keep calm. If he got too agitated and turned into his full demon form, I would have no chance of overpowering him. Even right now, he was stronger than me. I was human, although my blood was contaminated, and I was no match for a demon.

But an out-of-control demon who was young and fighting in a rage because I took his girl? Maybe I had a chance.

Mike wouldn't storm into the building like Cade did. Mike would take only controlled and well-thought-out steps and would measure each move before making it.

They both had a weak spot.

Twisting out of Cade's flailing grip, I removed my gun from my waistband, cocked it, and brought it up to face Nikki in one smooth motion. Cade stopped.

"Get in the cage," I said. He lifted a lip and snarled at me, the animal he truly was peeking through more and more. "Get in the *fucking cage.*"

When he didn't move, I fired a shot at Nikki's feet. To her credit, she didn't scream, only leaped backward in surprise and looked helplessly at Cade. Moving sideways, stepping one foot over the other, I unlocked the cage that held Nikki while keeping the gun trained on her.

"One move..." I muttered to her, "... one wrong move, and I'll kill you."

Nikki retreated to the back of the cage, and Cade stalked toward it, a constant growl rumbled through his throat. When he came level with me, he snapped his teeth at me through the air. I didn't flinch. I'd seen worse, only tightened my finger on the trigger. The movement caught his eye, and with another snarl, he stepped into the cage. The second he crossed the threshold, I slammed the door shut, and the moment the lock clicked into place, Cade was at the bars, swiping at me and snarling like the trapped beast he was. I stepped back, a half-smile twisting my lips, and Cade turned on Nikki, embraced her, and crushed her against his chest. I felt a hint of irritation that I had put them in the same cage, as now she had comfort, but torturing Nikki would be even more fun now there was a witness who cared.

Cade brushed his fingers through her hair, and they said nothing. They simply looked at each other and probably exchanged some wordless communication. A moment I was all too glad to interrupt.

"Funny," I said, pacing in front of the cage. "We both chose demons." Nikki only looked at me, unsure what I wanted her to say. Cade turned and snarled again, dragging Nikki closer to him and shielding her the best he could from me with his body. I tapped the barrel of the gun against my chin, still warm from the warning shot. "What's even funnier is that you two never bonded."

Cade's shoulders stiffened, and Nikki's grip on the back of his leather jacket tightened.

Looks like I'd found a sore spot.

"I wonder why that is. I'm sure a big, possessive male such as you would have wanted to bond with someone you loved so much. So that must mean it's my little sister who's holding out. What's the problem, Nikki, don't love him enough?"

"I love him very much," she mumbled. She knew exactly what I was doing, but she simply couldn't let even the implication she didn't care about Cade hang in the air.

"What's even more interesting is I don't need you two to be bonded in order to control him."

Cade was trying to hold Nikki back, to continue to shield her from me with his body, while she was desperate to ask the questions that were popping up in her mind, wondering what I'd done.

"What are you talking about?"

"Surely, you know if a demon loves someone,

their partner's blood becomes a weakness?"

She stilled, and Cade did too, his shoulders heaving. He looked around, taking in the cage around him.

"Son of a bitch," he muttered, glancing at his hands previously wrapped around the bars and the blood that now stained them.

I licked my lips before grinning, the discomfort the realization was causing him was permeating the air. He willingly got into the cage, and I suspect he imagined he would be able to turn into his demon form and break out.

But not while her blood was on every bar that surrounded him.

It's interesting, the things I learned in the early days when I was drilling Mike to tell me everything he could about demons and their lives and these rules that they all seemed to instinctually be aware of. Who would have thought demons were capable of love? But not only are they capable, they feel it stronger, with an intensity that would stagger humans. Their lover becomes their weakness long before bonding is even on their mind. If their partner is injured and they smell the blood and the pain, they will be brought to their knees.

And if you draw a circle around a demon with their love's blood, they can't step out of it.

So if you take the blood of their love and paint it across the cage's bars, they are trapped in their human form.

Cade started searching Nikki, shoving up her sleeves, and when he found the needle mark in the crook of her elbow, he roared in rage again, Nikki petting his arm gently as if to control a wild animal. She attempted to hide her own emotions and failed.

"Are you seeing this behavior, Nicola? Are you scared you'll turn into a monster like him if you bond?"

Nikki shook her head. I could see the movement of her hair that fell across his arm as he tucked her against him. Cade again tightened his grip on her. If he kept that up, he'd squeeze her to death before I had a chance to have my fun. "A monster like you, you mean?" she quipped, pushing Cade's arm down slightly so she could look me in the eye.

My smile dropped.

"Yes." My tongue darted out, wetting my suddenly dry lips. "That's exactly what I mean."

"It's none of your fucking business why we aren't bonded." Cade growled, turning his head to face me and his eyes flashing with rage. "Fuck off, or I'll rip your fucking heart out."

"From inside a cage of her blood?"

He hissed at me, his jaw taut as he contained himself, as if he had a choice, and I regarded him without response. As I moved away to finish setting the traps to contain Mike once he moved in on this building, Mike's lover boy stirred, groaning and clenching his fingers against the concrete under them.

I smirked to myself.

I'd be dealing with him soon enough.

CHAPTER
21

MIKE

There was a part of me that felt I could talk my way out of this, but Emrick couldn't be talked into waiting outside when we pulled up next to the remains of his club, Darkside. Ray and Ilsa agreed, reluctantly, to wait, but only when I asked them to keep an eye on the perimeter. While I would have thought Tate would've wanted to work alone, he had already secured the help of Earl, and therefore I didn't trust him not to have hired some random muscle to make things more difficult.

I also didn't trust Emrick not to fly off the handle. He didn't strike me as particularly stable, and even walking beside him felt like walking next to a ticking time bomb or an animal that couldn't be controlled. Ironic that as a demon, I should be concerned about an angel, fallen or not, not to keep control of himself.

Would he disregard Jacob's safety if there was an opportunity to take down Tate?

The husk of the building was lit, streams of artificial yellow lighting spewing forth from the cracks and holes where the fire had burned out the structure. The mild hum of generators was consistent in the background, and when the sound triggered in my mind the planning that Tate had put into this, I felt another push against the inside of my skin.

My demon wanted out.

I hadn't satiated its need for violence in too long. I'd lost my outlet, I'd almost lost Jacob, and now I was almost losing control.

The first thing I saw when we turned a corner was the cages planted strategically in what would have been a dance floor. In one, a woman with white-blonde hair was crouched down and curled her hands over her head. She was drenched, the drips from her clothes creating steady ripples in the puddle she stood in—an inch or two of water contained by the bottom of the cage. Standing over her, watching us approach, was Cade, his lips lifted into a snarl. He was also drenched but paying it no mind as he rested a palm on the head of the woman at his feet.

There was another cage, and...

"Jacob!" I cried out, my strangled shout a far cry

from the dominating and confident man I thought I was only a week ago. Emrick's hand shot out and grabbed my arm, and immediately I moved to shake him off, stopping when I heard the chuckle.

Tate stepped into the light, holding a trigger of some kind, wires spilling out and falling to the floor. Opening my mouth to ask, I instead followed the wires with my gaze as they led to the cages, metal and highly conductive, rigged up to send electricity pulsing through the bars.

And straight through the water his victims were standing in.

He'd taken their shoes.

Jacob's eyes met mine, and the look of utter despair in them shattered my heart. When I moved toward him, Emrick's grip on my arm tightened, and Tate laughed again.

"Not one step closer, lover, or they'll fry in front of you."

A nerve jumped in my cheek, but otherwise, I stopped, letting my eyes yellow and hoping I could halt him with only a look. I didn't want this to resort to violence, but he was holding Jacob's life above my head as I knew he would, yet somehow naïvely hoped he wouldn't.

"Tate," I said as Emrick's hand slid from my arm, his dark gaze on Tate and fingers twitching, itching to take his life. "We can talk."

"Sure." A smile lit Tate's face, and I almost

flinched. No humor, happiness, or love was there, only the darkness that lived within him, so deeply rooted it took up every part of him, brought to the surface by me. "Let's talk. While I've got you here, a captive audience, there are some things I'd like to tell you." His teeth flashed in the light as he grinned wider. "Might as well start by torturing you emotionally."

"Let Jacob go, and we'll talk."

"No. We'll talk now." He turned to Emrick. "A little surprised to see you here, *boss.*"

"You have your buddy Earl to thank for that."

Tate scowled but said nothing further about Earl, aware he'd been set up but so confident he had the upper hand, I doubted he cared much. He *did* have the upper hand—he held innocent people hostage.

And all because of me.

"Tate," I said, hoping that if I kept saying his name, it would reach a deep part of him that he'd forgotten, a more human part. "I'm sorry for how everything turned out. I'm sorry for what I did to you, and you deserved better than me."

He scoffed. "You think you're so fucking high and mighty. You're a demon who refuses to be a demon, who insists on hiding and suppressing the very thing that makes you better than everyone else. After what you put me through, the pain of the severance, I was waiting. Waiting for the perfect time to prove to you that you were no better than any other demon, that under the right circumstances, you were just as animal and out of control as the rest of them. You should have embraced it. We could have been so good together."

"Tate—"

"I've done a lot of fucked-up things, Mike, but even I never tore men limb from limb and left them to bleed out."

My mouth was dry, and I refused to clutch onto Emrick next to me even though the room had started to spin. I risked a glance at Jacob, and his face was whiter than before, terror ebbing through the dread. He was looking at me as the monster I truly am, the monster I tried to hide from him. No amount of getting closer, of sharing moments and happiness, could have braced him for the idea that I murdered humans.

But how did Tate know?

As if reading my mind, Tate said, "You're wondering how I knew about the men at the drug lab?"

But I couldn't answer. I simply shook my head, stuck between stepping away from Tate and wanting to move closer to Jacob, to drag him away from all of this.

Tate continued, clearly enjoying every second of it. "You were already losing control that night. I don't know what the fuck you used to do to control your demon, but I don't think it was working as well as you thought. Stumbling through the streets, halfway between demon and human, muttering and slashing at the air, I found you. At first, I didn't think you recognized me, but on some level, you must have, my scent at least, and you went ballistic. A severed bond was still a bond, and I don't think I've ever been so thrilled to be dragged into an alleyway. We fucked, Mike, like we should have been fucking all along... rough and dangerous and with blood. It was fucking glorious. Afterward, I managed to get you into my truck, and I drove you out to one of Emrick's furthest suppliers, his cooks, where we wouldn't be disturbed, and I let you loose on them."

My blood ran cold, and I felt Emrick's eyes on me. "Why?" was the only word I could choke out.

"Two birds with one stone. I got rid of one of Emrick's labs, something he had no explanation for, another seed in destroying the businesses' faith in his abilities, and..." his eyes yellowed, and I repressed a shudder, "... I proved that you were no better than any other demon. You're a killer, an animal, nothing more than a monster. I wanted you to be sent back to Hell. Imagine my surprise when you weren't."

Emrick growled. "It doesn't work like that, human."

"What?" Tate barked at him.

Emrick's lip curled into a sadistic grin, smirking as if privy to some sick irony or joke he wasn't sharing. He glanced briefly at the ceiling of the building and chuckled. "An out-of-control demon isn't responsible for human deaths. A demon is only punished for killing a human if it's a conscious decision, and they *choose* to take a life. That's the difference." He turned to me. "You harbor so much guilt for something you had no control over, and that was your savior."

"No matter," Tate said, waving the trigger around before smirking at me, "You had that broken memory with you, the guilt of what you had done, and that's an even better torture."

"I didn't know," I pleaded. I wanted Jacob to understand that I wasn't a monster, and I'm no longer what I used to be. I *needed* him to understand that I would *never* kill a human willingly.

Never again.

"Jacob, please, you have to believe me. I wasn't in control. I would *never* do that. Please..." but he was simply staring at me, eyes wide and unmoving, watching the scene unfold before him. His torture and pain were mine, and every second I felt myself coming apart at the seams. "I'm bound by the rules. If I had killed those men on purpose, I wouldn't be here." The emotions were too much, and Tate was taking from me my second chance at love. The first time I had allowed myself to feel anything, and he had turned it against me. Rage was bubbling in my stomach with despair as I turned back to Tate. "*You're* the monster. You *chose* to condemn those men to death."

"You're right, I'm not bound by your rules." His smile was twisted as his gaze shifted from me to Jacob. "I can kill whoever I want."

CHAPTER 22

JACOB

Several things happened at once.

The lights shut off.

There was a cry of rage as someone attacked Tate.

The cage next to mine rattled once, then twice, and again.

It sounded like the man inside was throwing himself at the bars wildly, and he'd hurt himself if he weren't careful. The woman in the cage was screaming at him to stop, and Mike was calling out my name. I squeezed my eyes shut, thinking that, somehow, I was going to be electrocuted. Did Tate have a backup? But it didn't happen. I remained still, soaked to the bone and shivering from fear and cold, but alive. I should be relieved, but I don't think I had it in me to feel much of anything anymore.

This is all too much for someone to take. If it were just Mike and me in a quiet room with only each other's company, we could talk and sort this out. I could ask questions, and he could reassure me that the monster was not who he really was. But this was chaos, and all I could say for sure was that I was alive.

Opening my eyes, it took me a moment to adjust to the dim light. The building may be a shell, but we were still undercover, and only dapples of the remaining daylight came through.

Inside, my heart was in shreds.

Was Mike the one who had attacked Tate?

Was he okay?

Did I even care if he wasn't?

Of course, I cared, and I hated that I cared. Part of me wondered if he'd used some demon power shit to make me care, but was that even a thing? I couldn't ask. There was no time to ask, no time for questions or to adjust. There was me captive and Mike coming to rescue me.

My cage rattled violently as Mike hit the side of it, his eyes a wild yellow, darting around the room and back to me before settling on the lock that held the door tight. With a snarl, he grabbed the lock, his fingers elongated with more joints than they should have, and skin popping with dots of a deep black, a black that could only come from nothingness, the complete lack of light and hope. It was spreading over his skin, creeping through his veins and spilling out, taking over.

He was changing, and I was going to see the monster.

When the lock snapped as easily as if it had been made of plastic, he swung the door open violently, ripping it from its hinges and discarding it to the side. I flinched at the sound of it hitting the floor, the metal on concrete. There were sounds of a struggle behind Mike, but I couldn't take my eyes off him. He loomed over me, wild and uncontrolled, and continued to change into the worst part of him.

"Mike..." I whispered. *That worked in the movies, didn't it?* You talked to them and reminded the monster that they had humanity inside them.

But he didn't stop.

For the briefest of seconds, his eyes turned back to gray.

But it didn't hold, and his elbows popped, the joints jerking the wrong way before slamming back again, and large curved bone-like appendages forcing themselves through his skin from his elbows and the backs of his wrists. I tried saying his name again, but there was no change this time, not even a hint that Mike was in there somewhere.

In coming to save me, he had lost control.

I had done this to him.

Torn between wanting to reach out to him while I could still see his face, the man I knew, and wanting to cower against the bars behind me before I could decide what to do, Mike was slammed to the side.

Tate came at me, brandishing a blade.

I had no chance.

He reveled in the moment the blade penetrated my torso, pulling it out with equal vigor and swinging it over his head in an arc before moving to bring it back down. Droplets of my blood flew off the blade, and I watched them in slow motion, transfixed and barely feeling the second stab.

Where was Mike? He said he would always take care of me and protect me. In slow motion, the blade came down for a third strike, and I wanted to tense before the impact, but the strength of my muscles was waning and beyond my control. The impact never came as Tate was thrown from me, and Mike and Emrick were inside the cage, moving around each other in the space not designed for so many. Mike was back in his human form, back to the man I let myself feel something for.

Back to protect me.

Turning my head to the side, I watched as Emrick wrestled with Tate over the blade. Emrick was laughing, and the sound was dark and disturbing. "I knew you'd be a fighter." He gyrated his hips obscenely, and Tate cried out in rage.

"You're such a sick fuck!"

Mike attempted to clamber over Tate and Emrick

to get to me, and Tate snatched at his arm. Everyone was a tangle of limbs and violence, and my vision was hazy. I couldn't make sense of it.

"I'll never stop, lover. You know that…" Tate crooned, grabbing at Mike and not letting go. His expression was manic, a wildness to his eyes beyond the yellowing, "… and you can't kill me."

Emrick snatched the blade from Tate's grip, and Tate's eyes widened, ignoring the chaos surrounding him as he realized…

He had lost.

"No." Emrick chuckled, sliding the blade along his tongue, still wet with my blood as he held Tate down. "But *I* can." Tate cried out as Emrick drove the blade into his chest, cutting long and deep, blood rushing from the wound and joining the water on the floor. Bile rose in my throat as I watched Tate's chest cavity open under Emrick's violent treatment before a warm hand touched my cheek as Mike turned my face to his.

"Mike…" I whispered, wincing at the pain of being moved. "You're human."

Mike looked at his hand briefly before pressing it to my wound, making me flinch. I groaned, but the room was spinning, and I couldn't manage much more than that.

"I don't understand," he said, shaking his head.

Emrick's face swam into view, streaked with blood, as were his teeth. My thoughts were confused. Wasn't he an angel? Even a fallen angel shouldn't be more terrifying than a demon. Emrick pointed upward to the bars. "Jacob's blood is on these bars, surrounding you. That's why you didn't finish the transformation."

"What does that mean?" Mike asked, his voice laced with desperation and confusion.

Emrick stared at Mike, his expression unreadable. "It means you love him."

He loves me?

Mike's face came into clarity as he stared at me. He was trembling, and I wanted to tell him not to cry, that I would be okay. But all I could manage was a weak smile. At least, I think that's what I managed. I couldn't be sure.

Everything felt numb.

Everything was spinning and fading.

He loves me?

He saved me.

He loves me.

We saved each other.

Everything went black.

CHAPTER 23

TATE

Mike moved above me, and I smirked as I coughed blood onto my chest. I'd managed to drag myself toward the back of the cage but slumped against it. I was dying. Fucking Emrick had killed me. I glared at him, and he stared back. No remorse, no expression, but a glint in his eye that reflected my hatred of him back at me. If I had known that fucker was going to tag along, I would have assembled the army I'd been creating to bring him down. Emrick was never a team player, and I had no reason to believe he would get involved.

Fucking Earl.

There were noises in the background. I couldn't place them, and it sounded like my sister was screaming. What was she carrying on about? I wasn't doing anything to her, though I tried. A cage was rattling, not this one. I couldn't feel anything. Voices. Was that Ray? Fucking hell, that bitch was everywhere. Fuck this. I didn't care enough to try to sort out the confusion of shit going on around me. Nothing mattered anymore. I'd failed, fucking abysmally. Fuck this.

I coughed.

I may have a demon's blood in me, but I was still human.

Fuck.

"Would you have killed me?" I asked, and Mike watched me. Emrick was tending to Mike's lover, having reassured Mike that he would be okay, that it was mostly shock, and I cursed internally. I didn't even get to kill *him*. This entire plan went to shit all because that fucker, Earl, dragged Emrick into this. *Was it a setup?* I'd never know. Earl was loyal to no one, after all.

Mike shook his head. "I never wanted to hurt you. Why did you do all this?"

I reached up, ignoring the tremble of my arm, and ran my fingers down Mike's face, leaving a trail of blood. "To show you that when pushed, you're no better than me."

Mike's face disappeared from view as he was shoved to the side, everything was blurry beyond my immediate vision, and when Nikki's face came into focus, I cursed, scowling at her, trying and failing to spit blood into her face. Her look of disgust told me she knew my intention.

"Where's Cole?" she asked, grabbing my shoulders. My head lolled to the side, and it took me a moment to understand what she was asking. "Where's the man who killed our father? Where did he go? I know you know!"

She was shaking me, and no one was stopping her. No one was crying out *no, please, you'll hurt him more* because no one cared. Not even me. I simply let her shake me. Blood gurgled from my mouth and dribbled down my chin as I chuckled.

"He'll kill you," I managed.

"Why do you care?"

I wanted to laugh, but it got caught in my throat. Nikki was watching me so intently. Did she feel anything for my dying? I had never given her a reason to care about me. Unlike our father, I wasn't able to switch between the darkness that was needed for the business into the role of a loving family member. I never really cared to try.

"You're my sister." I chuckled. "You're mine to kill."

"Where is he?" Nikki demanded with another shake of my shoulders.

Should I tell her? I'd never get another chance. She was only alive until today because of me. Cole could have killed her years ago, but I asked him not to because she was mine, *mine to kill.* She'd survived beyond her meddling only because I willed it. Now I was the one dying, and I never got to kill her. Maybe if she went after Cole, he'd finish the job. He'd killed our father when he lost the protection of his business when Emrick had taken it over, and Cole killed Dad simply because he could. But he didn't go after Emrick, or his territory, because Emrick was too strong, and this city wasn't worth it. So Cole moved on to somewhere he had more control. Regardless of who and what our father was, Nikki was, for some reason, strangely loyal to him and finding his murderer.

"Vegas," I muttered. I don't care why she thought I was answering. If it was some hope at redemption, or if I was offering her some fucked-up olive branch by giving her the current location of our father's murderer. I hoped Cole killed her, or maybe they'd even kill each other. That would be best.

I felt every heartbeat now as if my body was clinging to the feeling, trying to make it last a bit longer. Was my heart slowing down, or was it time? I couldn't be sure. Where was Mike? I wanted to take him with me into the abyss. Would I meet him in Hell one day?

Would I meet my father?

Nikki was shaking me again. Was she saying something or just shaking me? I couldn't make out the words. I couldn't tell. I hoped I was smiling at her. I hoped she had to watch the smile on my face as the light in my eyes dimmed.

I hoped the image haunted her forever.
I hoped she…

CHAPTER 24

MIKE

Jacob's blood saved me from my transformation. As long as I stood within this cage, I could hold onto my humanity. But Jacob needed to get to a hospital, so I would need every ounce of my strength to get him there.

My first thought was to transfer my ability to heal to him. I'd never done it before, but I knew how. However, Jacob was human, and the transfer only worked from one celestial to another. I cast a lightning-fast glance at Tate's body. He had demon blood in him, *my* blood, and I could have possibly healed him. With the extent of his injuries, the effort it would take to heal him, considering he is a bonded human and not a demon, would likely have killed me. Jacob's face was pale, and the muscles in my neck strained as I held myself together. He needed help and not the sort of help I could give.

I knew then I would have easily given my life to save Jacob, but I wouldn't do it for Tate.

Did that make me the monster he claimed I was?

Shaking the thoughts from my head, I needed to take action. I'd have to do something I hated doing and ask for help. With a few well-practiced flicks of my thumb over my phone, I texted Frank our location and a single word.

Urgent.

He would be here soon, and I could trust him to keep me controlled until Jacob was safe.

Tate was dead, and his body lay there, open-eyed and grinning, mocking me even in death. This isn't how I wanted things to go. Emrick seemed unconcerned with having taken Tate's life, and from the arch of his brow, I could tell he was wondering why I cared.

I cared because I wasn't on Earth to take lives or make them worse for anybody.

Yet, look at all the damage I had done.

Emrick shifted out of the way as I kneeled next to Jacob again. Emrick had torn off and tied his tank top around Jacob's torso, and Jacob's breathing had steadied, but he had not regained consciousness.

I loved him, and I hated myself for it.

Look at what had happened with Tate. Whoever he was before we met, he was a thousand times worse because of me. I brought out the darkness in him and gave him the power to inflict damage on others.

I looked over at Cade clinging to his partner, Nikki, as if his life depended on it, and I suppose, in a way, it did.

Demons loved deeply, completely.

"Cade," Nikki whispered, and he shushed her and brushed at her hair. They'd been let out of their cage by Ray and Ilsa, although from the state of the metal, it looked as though Cade would've busted it open eventually through sheer willpower.

Nikki shook her head. "Cade, I want to bond with you."

"You don't have to—"

"I want to. You love me so much that even the essence of my blood can stop you using your full strength. I love you more than life itself, and…" she hesitated, biting her lip, "… would you like to have a family with me? A baby?"

"Are you kidding?" Cade pulled her against him, making her grunt before giving a watery chuckle. "I'd *love* to have a baby with you."

"Good…" she whispered, clinging to his back, "… because I'm already pregnant."

Cade made a sound somewhere between a growl and a moan before laughing and pressing his lips to hers. My chest ached as I watched, and I was happy for them. Cade was a better human than me, and he was probably a better demon than me too. He had chosen his mate well, and their bond would last. I could tell from the way they clung to each other.

There was the screaming of tires outside a moment before the pounding of feet as Frank came storming into the building. His nostrils were flared, and I could tell he was checking out the situation from the smell alone—blood, fear, more blood, and… a near change. His eyes honed in on mine, and I didn't look away, giving him a quick nod of acknowledgment.

Frank growled openly and harshly, but before I bothered to speak to explain something that could wait, I bundled Jacob into my arms, and any lecture Frank was about to give me about releasing my desires to control my demon died on his lips. Without a word, he turned and went back to his car, indicating for me to follow.

Ilsa rolled her shoulders. "Damn, all this fucked-up family shit is making me rethink lunch with my mom next week."

Ray's eyebrows shot up. "You're having lunch with your mom?"

"Yeah." Ilsa's smile was sly with a hint of shyness I'd never seen from her before. "It's been too long. Besides, I thought it was time she met my wife."

"We're not married."

"Bonded… same thing."

Ray was looking at Ilsa with such intensity I turned away as Ray whispered something about *consummating the marriage,* and I didn't need to hear any more. Briefly, I faced Emrick. "Thank you," I muttered, feeling I barely deserved his help, but I was glad he did what he did, if only for Jacob's sake. "For everything."

Emrick lifted a shoulder. "I'll be in touch. You can owe me."

I didn't want to mention that he had also wanted Tate killed and that we were working together, nor did I mention that Emrick had insisted on coming along, and I hadn't asked or dragged him. But that was a conversation for another day.

"I'll come see you for our bonus! Pretty sure I broke a nail shutting off the lights," Ray called before grunting as I can only assume Ilsa punched her for saying such a thing when I was carrying Jacob's unconscious body. I almost felt like smiling, another perfect bonded couple, well chosen, well suited. Maybe they would get married as well and have the human and demon bonds cemented. That would be nice for them.

But that life wasn't for me.

Footsteps behind me indicated everyone was going their separate ways, back to their own lives with their partners. Ray and Ilsa, probably hand in hand, and Cade and Nikki, likewise. Emrick back to his wife, Cara.

A life I would never have.

I would need to let Jacob go.

Frank had to sweet talk the nurse to allow me sit with Jacob for a little while as I wasn't next of kin, and she giggled and flushed under his ministrations. Any other day, I would have chuckled at the idea he was going to go home smelling like another woman, and no matter how subtle the scent, Charlotte would pick up on that and tear into him. She knew he would never cheat. That wasn't the issue, as even a human woman bonded to a demon becomes territorial, and the enhanced sense of smell makes even being near those of the opposite sex a trial.

I waited by Jacob's bedside until he started to come around. It would have felt wrong to simply dump him in the Emergency Room and leave, and also cowardly. The least I could do was explain to him why he wouldn't be seeing me anymore and why I simply couldn't fall in love again.

"Mike..." Jacob's voice was weak, and I shushed him gently as I brushed his cheek, watching my hand carefully for any sign of the change, but there was none. It turns out heartbreak is a decent suppressant as well.

"Shh... just rest. You're safe now. You're in

the hospital."

His head tilted in an attempt to nod, and then he simply watched me. I wanted to convey everything I needed to say without words, but it was impossible when what I saw in his eyes was hope.

He couldn't hope, not for me, not for us.

I swallowed heavily. "Jacob... we can't see each other again." He frowned, pouted, and tried to speak again. "No," I cut him off, leaning back slightly from the bed, already beginning to put distance between us as if I could trick myself into thinking that would make this easier. "Look what I created when I bonded with Tate. Whatever he was before me, he was only worse after. I caused him so much pain, and I can't do that to you."

"Do I get any say in this?" The defiance in his tone struck me, and I wanted to smile but couldn't find it within myself to do so.

"No," I muttered, brushing his cheek with my thumb, recoiling my hand as if burned. I shouldn't touch him—every touch was false hope I couldn't offer him. "I'm a demon, and I'm better off alone."

"But you love me, my blood..."

His eyes pleaded with me, and the ache in my chest grew. When the muscles on my back spasmed, I sat upright. I was going to lose control again.

"I can't love you," I said, standing. "It's better for you if I'm not around."

"But you *do* love me," Jacob whispered.

I wanted to touch his face, brush his arm with my fingertips, and take him in my arms and embrace his beautiful body in mine. I wanted to tell him that everything would be okay and we could be together, but the best I could offer was to watch him from a distance. Foolishly, I had started a bond with him, my scent was in his blood, and other demons would be able to smell that. Maybe I did owe Emrick a favor, after all, as I would need someone with the pull and manpower to make sure Jacob was watched over if I couldn't be there to protect him.

My breath hitched, and I hated the sign of weakness.

But I was a coward, after all.

"Yes, I do love you," I whispered, stepping away, "But I simply can't."

Staggering out of Jacob's hospital room, I fell against Frank. When Jacob called out my name, I let out a wail and stumbled again, moving toward the door. Frank was on my heels, ushering me out of the building as my shoulders popped and my eyes glowed.

This time, there would be no going back.

Frank grabbed my elbow. "Come with me."

"Where—"

"Don't ask stupid questions. We need to get this out of your system. We're going to fight it out."

"I can control it," I said, even as I stumbled again, my leg jerking from under me with another spasm.

"Bullshit, you're too far gone. You were too far gone before, and now you're *beyond* that." Frank sounded pissed, and I didn't blame him. Once again, I pulled him away from his bonded partner to deal with my bullshit. How is it that I was viewed as the mature one, the boss, the controlled one, when more than once Frank had come to save my ass? I was no good at being a demon or a human.

People relied on me, my business was flourishing, and I needed to keep that going for them. If all I could do was enjoy the luxuries on Earth and provide a better future for those who worked under me, then so be it. Although I don't know if any level of good deeds would be enough to cover the damage I had done. But it didn't matter. I had no mark anymore, and when I died on Earth, it would be for good.

Frank yanked me into an abandoned warehouse, and I was struggling too much simply to keep myself together to notice if this was or wasn't where the fight clubs were usually held. It was dark out, and I had no idea what time it was, not that it mattered. We were alone, and Frank wouldn't let me hurt anyone.

I could trust him, but the fear was real.

"Frank," I pushed the word through gritted teeth. "What if I try to…"

Frank was rolling up his sleeves. "I'm not going to let you fuck me, Mike."

How was he not afraid of the monster?

I guess because he was never ashamed of his.

Gritting my teeth against the roar threatening to escape, the transformation took over. My limbs and fingers elongated, my skin blackened until I was almost part of the shadows that surrounded us, save for the yellow of my eyes and the glowing red etching of demonic power that worked its way across my skin, crisscrossing with the scars from my severed bond—a lifetime reminder of Tate and what he had done, what I had created in him.

What I couldn't risk creating in Jacob.

The wind was knocked from my lungs as Frank launched himself head-first at me, and my feet slid across the concrete as he slammed me backward. Gripping his shoulders, I slowed his momentum until we were locked together. Frank had a great deal more fighting experience than I did, but he was in his human form, and I in my demon, and I had much greater strength than he this way.

In the handful of times I had attended the fight club under Frank's insistence following the incident at the drug lab, even then, I wasn't fully letting go of control. I think Frank knew that, but he knew better than to push his luck when it came to bossing me around. I was *at* the club, and that was a feat within itself. But this time, there was no control, not an ounce of me left inside telling me I needed to keep control because what was I keeping control for? I had lost Tate long ago, and then against my will, my heart had opened itself to Jacob. But I shut that door, and now he probably hated me.

It was for the best.

With another roar, this one I didn't attempt to muffle, I swiped my foot around Frank's leg, misbalancing, and crashed him to his back. As he went to stand, I leaned over him and began swiping, my claws in their full form sliced into his skin, and when I caught Frank across the face, he bellowed at me, "Not the fucking face!" But there wasn't anything in me to be amused by his obsession with his appearance, even at a time like this.

Frank's shirt was in shreds, his chest bleeding as he launched at me again. I fell under his weight and force, and he wrapped his fingers around my throat, using the hold to pummel my head against the concrete, each one drawing an angered growl from me.

The longer we fought, the less control I had, and my last sane thought before I became animal, consumed by rage, guilt, and self-loathing, was that

I hoped Frank knew what he was doing because he was the only one in control now.

CHAPTER
25

MIKE

My only sense that time had passed was the sunlight that broke through the warehouse, scattering across the floor and highlighting the debris, and now, the blood as it went.

"Someone is going to think there was a murder here." Frank's voice penetrated through the air and assaulted my eardrums. I hurt—everything hurt. The ache was all-consuming, but when I lifted my hand in front of my face, I could release a sigh of relief that it was back to human form. The cuts and bruises wouldn't take too long to heal, but I embraced the pain while I felt it.

Penance.

I took a quick mental scan of my body—maybe a couple of broken ribs, a dislocated shoulder, but mostly cuts and bruises. It's possible the cuts were self-inflicted in my frenzy, and I didn't even care about that. Lying on my side on the dusty floor, I huffed out a breath and groaned before lifting myself into a sitting position. Frank gave me only the briefest warning, "This is going to hurt." As he grabbed my arm and my neck, he roughly shoved my shoulder back into place. I roared and snarled and, on a lingering instinct, swiped at him. Frank simply grabbed my hand as I attacked him and pulled me to my feet.

Rolling my shoulder, it was back in position, and I glared at Frank as he returned to his phone, typing out a text.

"Is Charlotte mad you were out all night?" I asked.

"Nah," Frank said, finishing the message and shoving the phone back into his pocket. There wasn't much left of his shirt, and his black pants were so covered in dust they were almost white, darkened when our blood seeped through the fabric. "She understands, certainly more than she did last time."

Images appeared of Charlotte against the wall as I rushed her, on the edge and out of control, and how she'd whimpered when I'd pressed my body against hers seconds before Frank had ripped me away. When I had lost control, Charlotte had witnessed a demon at his most dangerous only shortly after discovering Frank's true nature. It must have been a lot for her, and I didn't need the reminder of the fear in her eyes. Fear I had caused.

I grumbled my acknowledgment, not in the mood to be reminded of my past indiscretions so soon after this one.

"How are you feeling?"

I stared at Frank, assuming he could only be asking about my physical condition. "I'm back in control." Then after a beat, added, "Thank you."

His eyes narrowed, and he spun on his heel and walked toward the exit. I followed, shoving my hands in what was left of my pants pockets, otherwise naked, my shirt having been shredded beyond saving. There was no danger in leaving our clothes and blood in the warehouse. The police couldn't classify or identify demon blood or DNA anyway.

Frank took a few turns around corners as I followed him, and I arched an eyebrow but said nothing. This was not the most direct way home, nor to his car which he had left at the hospital last night. Maybe he'd sent one of his lackeys to pick up the vehicle, and he was in the mood for a walk, but Frank rarely did anything without intent.

When we continued in silence, I finally asked, "Where are we going?"

"I'm going to show you something." And that was all he offered.

We turned a few more corners until it became

apparent that Frank was randomly moving. He was looking for something, but he didn't seem to know where it was. My frustration grew, and he shushed me whenever I tried to ask. This was the worst end of the city, and I didn't spend a great deal of time here, so I had no idea what he might be trying to find.

There was a scuffle and a muffled cry, and Frank's arm shot out and slammed across my chest, halting my movements as he tilted his head. Pressing his fingers to his lips, he beckoned for me to follow him, and when we rounded one last corner, there was a group of youth, men and women, surrounding a young woman who was pressed against the wall, whimpering as they chuckled at her distress.

"I think she likes it," one of the women in the group said, laughing. She had an almost permanent scowl on her face, but her joy at their victim's discomfort was evident in her eyes, bright with passion. I sniffed the air—humans—they were all humans, no scent of a demon near here. Glancing at Frank, I wondered how much longer he planned to watch this display without intervening. It wouldn't be the first time. I'd known him to interrupt muggings and attempted rapes on his way back from the fight club, acting as some sort of demon vigilante and brushing it off like it was no big deal. I liked that he looked out for humans, although I didn't always approve of the violence.

Although recently, I'd started to see the merit in its use as a control form for our demons.

Maybe I'd get him a cape just to fuck with him.

The group laughed again, and when one of the men approached the woman pressed against the wall and snaked his hand up her thigh, riding her skirt up, Frank shouted a simple, "Hey!"

The group turned, and I can't imagine that two men with shredded clothes would have been the most intimidating sight if it weren't for the addition of the blood and dust. The attackers stopped, assessing the threat as they backed away from their victim, and Frank lifted a lip in a scowl.

"Which one of you is going to serve as an example to the others?" he asked.

There was laughter again, albeit with much less enthusiasm. One of the larger men stepped forward, and the realization dawning in his eyes the closer he got to Frank and the difference in their size became apparent was, I'll admit, entertaining. But it was too late. He had singled himself out as the leader and to back down now would lose him credibility with his peers. The man shuffled his feet, lifting his fists in front of his face, showing he was ready to fight.

He couldn't be ready for Frank.

Frank snatched out at him, grabbing his throat and lifting him from his feet. The move took little to no effort, and the protests from the man's group were only verbal, no one keen enough to step forward and get involved. Frank pulled the man close to his face, and his tongue darted out, wetting his lips in anticipation.

He let his eyes slide to yellow, and the man panicked, grabbing Frank's arm and trying to leverage himself free of the grasp while gasping for air.

"Behave…" Frank growled, letting the dual tone of demonic power creep into his voice, "… or next time I'll kill you all. This city is *my* city, do you understand?"

The man choked out a reply, though I couldn't tell what it was. Frank repositioned his feet and launched the man over his group and down the alley. The group turned and ran, one of the men and one of the women stopping to lift their now-unconscious comrade and dragging him away. Frank turned to the victim, but she squealed in fright and grabbed her purse from the ground, keeping her head down and fleeing, brushing past me as she went.

Frank stood, arms crossed over his impressive chest, watching me.

My lip twitched in irritation. I didn't understand the purpose of his display. I knew of his strength. That's why he was the only one I thought of calling when I was losing control. His actions seemed an odd display after the events of the past few days, and I wanted to turn and walk away, not in the mood for his games and bullshit. All I wanted to do was get back to work and immerse myself into the life I had created here on Earth after Tate and before I knew what it was like to love again.

"Did you plan on wandering around all day until we found someone? How did you know there was an attack going on?"

Frank scoffed. "At this end of the city? There's *always* something going on. I just followed the fear."

"Why did you bring me here?" I demanded.

"Because humans can be fucked up," he said as if that answered all my questions.

"I know that, Frank. You think I don't know that?"

"No," he said, storming forward and closing the gap between us. He poked a finger into my bare chest over the scars of my removed mark. His eyes flickered to those new scars for a moment, and I know he knew what they were and what I had done. I imagined he'd be furious, but maybe he knew me well enough to understand why I had done what I did.

Because I didn't want to go back to Hell.

I never wanted to go back.

I'd rather be dead.

"I don't think you *do* understand, Mike. Because all these years you've been blaming yourself for

Tate and what he *became* after the bonding. But that's all *bullshit.* You were so caught up in trying to be the perfect human you've completely missed the point."

Anger was bubbling in my stomach, and I gritted my teeth, ignoring the urge to shove his finger away from my chest. "And that is?"

"That you're *not* human, Mike, and you never fucking will be. You shouldn't even want to be. You're a fucking demon, for fuck's sake! Be proud of it. And here's the thing, no—" he cut me off as I opened my mouth to retaliate. "You don't get to speak… this is where you listen. I've seen some self-destructive bullshit in my time, Mike, but I've never seen *anyone* who hated themselves as much as you do. I've never seen anyone so intent on blaming themselves for other beings' actions that they locked themselves up tight and refused to truly live." He sucked in a deep breath with a look that warned me not to interrupt. When he continued, his tone was gentler. "Whatever Tate was after you bonded, that was in him *before* you bonded. From our decades in Hell, how did you never learn that people do messed-up shit? That humans can be the worst of the worst, without remorse, without caring for their fellow beings? Tate was a monster long before you got to him."

My top lip lifted into a scowl because somehow the expression helped me hold back the tears threatening to break free, and there was no fucking way I would cry in front of Frank. As if he didn't think I was already so much of a fuck-up, I wouldn't confirm it by completely breaking down at his feet. He'd told me this before, that Tate must have been dark before the bonding, but I could never accept it because there's one part of that which never made sense to me.

I swallowed and looked away from Frank for long enough to blink away the emotion and then held his eye contact again so I could finally verbalize it. "Why couldn't I see it?" I whispered.

Frank sighed. "You were young and blinded by fresh feelings in a new world. Earth is a lot to take in, with a fuckton of novel sensations that can be completely intoxicating. You should know that's something I know better than most." He threw me a significant look before continuing, the edge gone from his voice. "You were young, Mike, and you didn't see him for what he truly was. You were too busy hating yourself to know that it was never love with Tate. He was the first human to accept your demon, something even *you* couldn't do. You can't blame yourself for falling for him. Love can blind us."

"What if I make the same mistake again?"

"You won't."

We stared at each other for a long moment. I don't think I could ever forgive myself for how things turned out with Tate, and although I knew Emrick wanted him dead anyway, it didn't help my conscience to know I led him right to him. Tate was hurting, but Tate was also vengeful and became consumed by it.

That part wasn't my fault.

I nodded, acknowledging to Frank that I was at least attempting to absorb his words, and I was trying to believe them. I wanted to believe them. Maybe with time, I would.

"When did you get so damn smart?" I asked, glaring at him.

Frank let out a bark of laughter, clapping me on my shoulder. "Mike, I was always smarter than you. You just never admitted it."

CHAPTER
26

JACOB

Life is more precious now.

It was always precious, and I thought I was one of those people who stopped to smell the roses and all that touchy-feely stuff about being in the moment and enjoying the little things. Until my life was almost taken from me, and I was faced with the reality of demons and angels and an entire world of supernatural I didn't know existed beyond movies and books.

I couldn't stay in the city where all of that had happened.

Dad tried his best to understand, and it simultaneously broke my heart and made it swell with love to watch him try. He had a future lined up for me, a career, an entire life. But it wasn't the life I wanted, and I simply couldn't spend one more day existing in a world I didn't belong in when nothing was stopping me from taking control of my life.

I moved to San Francisco for one reason that made complete sense from a logical point of view and a second reason that was just for me. One, a friend of mine from my school days whom I had kept in touch with on and off due to our mutual love of classic cars lived there. Apparently, there were several events throughout the year, and he had contacts who could help me get my own garage up and running.

Secondly, because of the famous car chase from the film *Bullitt.* A 1968 Ford Mustang and a 1968 Dodge Charger screaming through the streets of San Francisco, how could I resist the pull? Somehow, I doubted I could get away with going one hundred and ten miles per hour through the Marina, but it was nice to dream.

Mike would smirk at the idea of me choosing a location for a new life, at least partially based on the city's car chase film history.

It had been three months, and I hadn't forgotten him.

In fact, far from having forgotten him, he was often at the forefront of my mind, and I could see his face so clearly—an arrogant, serious expression which was his default, with eyes that spoke more than words ever could. But then I would say something or do something just to make him laugh, to break the façade, and he would, and it would change his whole face. I loved the lines around his eyes and the gray hair, and I loved that when he finished laughing, he would pierce me with those gray eyes, and they would flash with lust.

Then sometimes in my mind, those eyes would shift to yellow.

And in those moments, I'd expect to feel a twinge of fear. But there was no fear, the only one who made me afraid was Tate, and he was gone now. He was human, and he had been more of a threat to me than the demons I had apparently been around ever were. Although Emrick, I was afraid of him, he felt like darkness personified, the complete opposite of Zaqiel. Hard to believe they were both angels.

Hard to believe angels were living in my hometown and just... being.

I'd somewhat expected a call from Mike, but apparently he wasn't messing around when he was determined to keep space from me. Several times I had punched in his office number, then hung up when his secretary answered. Fuck knows what I would have done if he had answered. I've dated no one since moving here—it was kind of hard when you were comparing everyone to a demon.

A tentative, caring, protective, and funny demon who was fucking amazing in bed.

Shaking the thoughts from my head, I got back to work. Right now, my garage was only me, but once my reputation of my work had spread through the classic car community, the bookings were piling up, and I didn't think it would be long before I needed to hire some help. Finding someone I trusted enough to work on these babies unsupervised would be difficult, so perhaps I would start my search within the very community that had been so welcoming to me. Who better to work next to than someone who was equally as much a fanatic and detail-oriented as me?

Wiping the back of my hand across my forehead, I laughed out loud when I felt the oil slick across my skin. Glancing down at my overalls, I laughed again. I was filthy, and I loved picturing my father's face, comparing me now to the me he knew in suits and incredibly shiny shoes.

Gently closing the hood with a click, I dumped my tools on a nearby bench and slid into the driver's seat, making sure to sit only on the paper covering I had placed on the floor and seats to stop from getting them dirty. Turning the key in the ignition, the Mustang roared to life then settled into a rumbling purr, the familiar sounds reverberating through the garage and making me sigh in contentment. Flicking it off, I stepped out of the vehicle and patted the hood lightly before putting the keys away in my office and locking the place up. It was past seven o'clock, but I had nowhere to be and absolutely did not mind working late.

Stripping off my overalls, I sighed again, and this time only the silence of the garage echoed around me. Once the radio was off and all the cars were done with for the night, I was alone.

But in so many ways, I was alone.

I'd planted the seeds for the start of an excellent life here, and while I loved every minute, there was a constant niggling feeling in my mind and chest.

Because I fucking missed Mike.

It was stupid and irrational, and I hated that I still felt for him. But the simple truth is the feelings never went away. He did nothing but try to protect me and ultimately decided he needed to safeguard me from himself as well. Yet, in the entire messed-up situation, he was the only one I ever felt truly safe with. I was untouchable with Mike. No one could hurt me because Mike wouldn't let them. I could be me and unapologetically me, and he was encouraging and kind and witty and every fucking good word I associated with someone I wanted to spend my life with.

But he had made the choice for both of us.

I paused, half-expecting a romance-movie moment where he walked through the door, telling me he had come to get me back and never stopped loving me. I *knew* he loved me because of some demon bullshit I still didn't fully understand, but I had somehow helped him keep control.

There was nothing but the sound of passing

cars outside.

Sighing and trying desperately to regain the sense of serenity I had only moments before, I finished locking up, set the alarm, and left. My car— my girl—was in my garage, but I needed to clear my head, and what better way to do that than the typical walk home. San Francisco was a mystery to me. Everyone here seemed to know their place and simultaneously felt like they were all trying a bit too hard. At least, that's how it felt to me, but perhaps I was simply projecting myself onto everyone around me.

Almost home, I passed a newspaper stand and, by habit, scanned the front page of the paper and magazines as I passed. I didn't have a chance to do this most mornings, the vendors were up early, but I was up earlier and often didn't walk.

I stopped dead in my tracks.

Because Frank's smug mug was looking up at me from an architecture magazine, arms crossed and grinning as though he knew what everyone was thinking.

Behind him, the title *Blackman, Conner, and Associates expand to San Francisco.*

Oh, you have got to be fucking kidding me.

There wasn't a chance in hell I could stay away.

Pulling my phone from my pocket, I frantically opened a search engine and found the address of their new office. It wasn't near here. Of course, it wasn't, this was not the spot for high-end businesses like that.

It was, however, a short cab ride.

Fuck it. I had to know.

Hailing a cab, I jumped in and gave them the address, too nervous and filled with excitement to realize I hadn't put my seat belt on until the driver gently reprimanded me, his eyes meeting mine in the rearview mirror. He may have asked if I was okay. I couldn't be sure because there was nothing on my mind now but Mike. The scent of him, the feel of his hands on my body, and the way he made me feel inside, everything was overwhelming me as every memory of every sensation came back all at once and stronger than ever.

We pulled up outside the building, and I swiped my card to pay the driver, declining a receipt and bounding out of the vehicle and up the stairs, halting at the doors.

Would he even be here?

Maybe he sent Frank?

I had come rushing over here like some romantic fool, but what would I even say?

My fingers drummed against my upper thigh as I stood by the front doors. The building was open, and when I took some steps backward and glanced up, the occasional window was lit with a late-night worker getting in some final hours as the evening closed in. Evidently, I loitered out the front for too long, and the security guard came outside and walked toward me.

"Everything okay here, sir?"

I almost smirked. *Sir* was said with a tone that implied he was purely being polite but made clear he felt I shouldn't be here at all. "I'm here to see an old friend," I blurted out, immediately correcting my tone as I continued, "It's been a while. I'm nervous."

"Who are you here to see?"

"Mike Conner."

"It's after office hours, but if you give me your name, I can call up."

Hesitating, I nodded slowly and followed him to his desk, where he punched something into the panel. The second Mike's voice came through the small speaker, I tensed, then relaxed, then tensed again. I wanted to pace or run up the stairs or run away, but I needed to get moving because standing still was torture.

"Yes, Eric?" Mike said, voice slightly crackling at the beginning of the question with static.

"I have someone here to see you... says he's an old friend."

"Who is it?"

The guard looked at me. "Who are you?"

"Jacob Macintyre."

Eric went to repeat the name, and Mike's voice crackled through, "I heard."

There was silence, and Eric looked at me, the silence growing awkward. "Shall... shall I send him up?" Eric questioned.

There was more silence, then finally, achingly. "Yes."

"Very well, sir." The *sir* he gave Mike was genuine, and so he should. Mike deserved his respect. Eric pointed to the elevators to my left and handed me a swipe card. "Swipe this, then level twenty-two. Bring the card back on your way out."

Nodding, I accepted the card as he scribbled my name in a sign-in book, my hand trembling as my fingers closed around the plastic, and I shuffled my way to the elevator. All my nervous energy seemed to have diminished into simply nerves, and I paced the elevator car as it moved smoothly upward, using the last few seconds to check my hair in the mirror.

"Shit," I muttered, seeing the giant smear of grease on my forehead. No wonder the guard was looking at me funny. "Shit, shit." As I went to wipe it, the smear only increased, thinning it out but taking up a larger section of skin. I was still muttering and wiping at my face when the elevator dinged politely, and I rushed out before the doors closed, moving down the hallway and through a glass door with the company name proclaimed in elegant black text.

The office was silent, and unsure where to go, I

took a few tentative steps in.

Man, how did I work in places like this? Just being back in an office made me feel out of place.

"Jacob."

I stopped and turned, seeing Mike at the end of the hallway. His voice was smooth and dark, and I trembled slightly, excitement once again pulsing through me. I'd forgotten what his voice could do to me. He beckoned me, and I walked toward him, trying not to look as nervous as I felt. Why was I even nervous? He had left *me.* But that was just the point, wasn't it? Mike had left *me.* Was I in some way ignoring his wishes by showing up when he had already made his position clear?

Mike didn't look angry, and his neutral expression turned into a smirk as I approached, his eyes flickering to my forehead. The moment struck me as so obscure I simply grinned back, my shoulders relaxing as I followed him, stepped into his office, and sat in one of the luxurious chairs opposite his desk. I expected him to move around the desk and sit in his chair, but instead, he came and sat in the chair next to me, on the edge and leaning forward to rest his elbows casually on his knees. He studied me for a moment, and I was pleased there was no malice in his eyes, no anger at my being here, only curiosity and a hint of sadness.

"I missed you," I blurted out, and Mike's eyebrows shot up.

"I missed you too." The simple confession took my breath away for a beat, and I cleared my throat.

"I'm sorry I'm here. I know you told me you didn't want to see me—"

"Jacob."

"I mean, I feel in part like I'm pushing a boundary by ignoring your wishes, but when I found out you were here, I couldn't stay away. I had to come—"

"Jacob—"

"I've made a life for myself here, and I've been happy. But I could never stop thinking about you and what you really are… somehow that never even came into it? Because it's just you, it was always just you, and I like who I am with you. I—"

Mike saved me from myself and my ramblings by placing a hand over my mouth, and I almost moaned. "Jacob," he said again, removing his hand and slowly dragging his finger across my bottom lip before waiting, perhaps giving me another chance to interrupt. One of his eyebrows was arched in permanent amusement through my entire spill, and I couldn't help but smile at the expression. His face relaxed, and when he smiled back at me, everything else in the room simply disappeared. Because it was real, a genuine smile. He was different, and I could feel it.

"Your father told me you came here and that you're doing quite well. He's proud, you know."

"He is?"

"Of course he is. He's a success-driven man. Just because you didn't seek success in the same industry as him doesn't mean he doesn't recognize it for what it is."

"Did you come here because of me?" I breathed the words out because it seemed like such a ludicrous concept. To choose a location for your company's expansion based on the whereabouts of an old flame? No one would do that. No one except perhaps...

"It was Frank's idea," Mike said, and there was a twinkle in his eye, a spark of mischief. "It didn't hurt that we'd been discussing this as a potential location anyway, but when he found out you were here, it wasn't even a question anymore."

"Were you..." I swallowed heavily, Mike had inched forward in his chair, and his knees were brushing mine. He was searing hot and sending pulses of desire through me, making it harder to think. There were so many things we should talk about before we even thought of touching, but now that he was so close, I couldn't think of anything else but feeling him next to me. "Were you going to come looking for me?"

Mike's lip twitched into almost a smirk. There he was, the hint of arrogance, the swagger, the man who he could be if only he let himself. In the beginning, I wanted to be there for him as he went through his trauma to find himself, and although I had no idea how deep or how dark that trauma was, it made my heart skip to see him come out the other side.

Smiling and smiling for me.

"Eventually," he said, reaching out experimentally and brushing my leg. My gaze darted to his hand, and when I didn't stop him, he left his hand resting there. I realized mine were frozen on my lap but couldn't find the power to make myself move. "When I had settled in more, and..." he grinned and winked at me, "... when I had worked up the nerve."

"You don't seem so nervous now."

"You do." I wanted to argue, but I couldn't. I could barely even string a sentence together because I was intoxicated by him. It was like meeting him for the first time all over again. He was power and grace and wonderfully, amazingly sexy. Mike reached up and brushed my cheek before running his thumb along my lower lip again. I parted my lips, inviting him to do more, and his eyes flashed with lust. "Do you have anywhere to be tonight?" I shook my head, finally managing to reach out and run my hand up Mike's thigh, making him shudder. "Want to break in my new office?"

"Wha—" I realized what he meant the nanosecond the syllable left my lips. Mike quirked a brow, and I leaned forward, grabbing his face and planting a kiss on his lips. "Yes," I breathed out, "Oh, fuck yes."

EPILOGUE

MIKE

It took a few months for me to get myself together enough to complete the bonding with Jacob. I explained to him, over and over, how it was intended to be permanent. If, for some reason, we didn't work or he grew to hate me or what I was, then the process to sever the bond was not only painful, but this time, it would likely kill me.

What I didn't tell him was that if it ever came to that, dying would be my desire. After everything else, losing Jacob would be too much. Maybe I would be a coward again, but I would take the ticket out. Knowing he would be left scarred, physically and emotionally, would be too much guilt for me to handle.

Yet every time we had the discussion, it ended the same way, with Jacob reassuring me he loved me and wanted to spend the rest of his life with me.

His life would be longer if we bonded, and he would be stronger and faster with hints of the power that I had. He was okay with this, and I simply couldn't see him using these powers for anything nefarious. Frank agreed, and when I tried to talk it over with him for the fourth time, he told me to *just fucking do it already,* and before he hung up, I heard Charlotte yell, "*We love you, Mike, really we do*" from the background a second before the call went dead. I know she could give a hard time as good as Frank could, and after that call, when I gripped the handset so hard it cracked, I hoped she gave him hell.

Three months after we moved in together, Jacob was waiting for me when I got home. We both worked a lot, and it was a gamble who would be home first. But his business was growing—he'd hired an assistant mechanic and was looking for another, and my new branch was up to fifteen employees and looking at another expansion soon.

Jacob greeted me, wearing nothing but jeans, a smirk plastered on his face that told me he was up to no good. I returned the look, and he peeled my fingers from my briefcase, placing it by the front door as he locked it. Without a word, he led me to the couch and straddled me.

"What's this about?" I whispered, running my hands up his back. I loved the way his skin exploded with goose bumps from my touch and how smooth his skin was as I gripped his shoulders.

"Maybe I just missed you."

"You always miss me, but that's not it. Something's different."

He leaned forward, tracing his tongue along my neck and over my throat, and my breath hitched when he passed over my Adam's apple. Jacob chuckled when I started breathing harder, and my grip on his back increased before I ran my hands down and cupped his ass, lifting him against me. His hips were grinding against mine, and of course, I was already hard. He was too.

"Jacob..." I warned as his teeth found my neck, and he bit gently, testing my reaction.

"Mike..." he mimicked my tone, and I could hear the smirk in his voice. I snarled. It was involuntary. Did he think this was a game? I still wasn't sure if he fully understood the powers he was dealing with. Could he ever really understand? We could talk and talk and go over the same ground a thousand times, and hell, he didn't even seem bothered now if my eyes flashed to yellow while we fucked.

But the guilt was there, lingering beneath the surface. Tate's face was etched in my mind and reminded me of all I had done and had the potential to do again. Jacob wasn't like Tate, I knew that, but it was near impossible to completely wipe the slate clean of all sense of responsibility when you had carried it for so long.

I ran my fingers through Jacob's hair and gripped it, pulling his face from my neck when he moaned. "What do you think you're doing?"

"Mike, I want you, and I want to be with you. I think we should finish this."

I knew the yellow had crossed over my eyes, and Jacob didn't even flinch, instead leaning forward to playfully bite my bottom lip. I snarled again. "What makes you so sure you can handle it?"

"I spoke to Charlotte."

"You did *what?*"

Why did that make me so angry? He had every right to talk to Charlotte. In fact, it made sense. She'd been where he was, and she had even less time to become accustomed to the truth of Frank's and my nature before it was thrown ruthlessly in her face, and she'd had no choice. Yet she still loved Frank, and they still bonded. I wanted what they had. I ached for it.

And Jacob wanted it with me.

Reckless was not me. I became more calculated as I got older, never taking a chance, always assessing everything. But I had been assessing this for months, so what more could come of it? Would time change how I felt about Jacob? No, I knew that to my very core. He understood the risks. He may be human, but he was capable of making his own choices.

And the fact that he chose me flared a possessiveness through me that presented itself in a growl. Jacob shuddered as I let my eyes turn into their natural yellow, with cat-like slits for irises. Dragging a nail across my skin, I cut into my chest.

"Do you want this?" I asked, my voice deep and ethereal.

Jacob's eyes never left mine. "Yes."

He had already tasted my blood once, accidental or not, and it had started the bond. Once more, he would be mine, and I would be his. Between demons, a bond required a two-way drinking of blood, but for humans, they only had to drink ours. If I were to taste Jacob's blood, my mind would be flooded with his worst and most traumatic memories, the parts of him that churned emotional turmoil within. Unfortunately, it was a side effect of being a demon and a trick we used to find out the secrets people wouldn't tell us in Hell so as to more effectively torture them.

Deepening the cut, I then increased my grip on Jacob's hair, his breaths coming in heavy gasps. His gaze was flickering between my eyes and my hand.

"Do it," I whispered because part of me believed he wouldn't, part of me still feared that none of this was real, that his love was fake and only on the surface. "If you want me, do it."

There was no hesitation, and I think that's when something in me snapped. My grip on his hair relaxed long enough for him to lower to my chest of his own accord, although my fingers flexed and released in his blond locks. The second his parted lips touched my chest, and his tongue darted out, taking the first droplet of my blood within him, I gripped his head and pushed.

"Take it," I snarled out, holding his mouth against my chest with one hand while undoing his pants with the other. With a bit of maneuvering, I managed to get them off one of his legs so I had access to his cock—he had gone commando, as always. He whimpered when I gripped him, working his cock as he drank my blood. My head spun as he swallowed and took another mouthful, the suction of his lips against my pectoral almost became too much.

I managed to keep myself in control just enough to know that I needed him to stop.

Using his hair, I pulled him from my chest, letting the wound flow freely—that would take care of itself—and moaned as Jacob licked a remaining droplet of blood from his lips.

"*Fuck,*" I murmured, keeping hold of his hair because I knew what was next.

He was human, and his body would fight the intrusion of my blood. He started shaking, and I kept my grip on his hair, shifting my other hand to his thigh. When he opened his eyes, they were a brilliant yellow, and for the briefest second, I recoiled in shock because my Jacob was no longer simply human, he was bonded to a demon.

Then the possessiveness flared again.

Not just any demon—*me.*

He was bonded to *me.*

He was *mine.*

I growled, and Jacob smirked, closing his eyes until the shuddering reduced. "Control yourself," I warned, and he frowned. When he opened his eyes, they were still yellow, though faded, and I could see his natural color through them. It took him a few minutes, taking time to close his eyes and focus each attempt until he finally opened his eyes and was the man I fell in love with.

"It feels…" Jacob lifted his hands to my shoulders, gripped and flexed, and paused when another growl rumbled through my throat at his touch. "I can't describe it."

"Try."

"Like my blood is thicker… like my heart has to work harder, but it's not uncomfortable. My eyes, though…" He closed his eyes again, tentatively touching his eyelids as though expecting to find something different than before, although he knew that even bonded humans didn't take on demon physical traits beyond the eye color. "My eyes are sensitive, and everything is clearer, crisper. I can feel my fucking eyelids on my eyes. It's so bizarre."

"It'll take time. I'll have to teach you control."

When he looked at me again, he was smirking. "*You're* going to teach *me* control?"

Snarling, I gripped his hair again, yanking his head back. "Is that a fucking problem?"

"No." He gasped, and I heard his heart rate increase with his arousal.

"Good." Because my demon was screaming for him to take him, my new bonded partner. Fucking wasn't necessary to cement the bond, but it sure as hell made it more fun. The instinct was there, strong and making itself known, and although I had been taking part in a fight club with the small yet present demon population in this city, and although Jacob and I had been giving in to our physical desires every chance we got, I was not prepared for the flare of need that would come when I smelled Jacob's skin and sweat, and beyond that, his scent was *mine.*

I bit into his neck, causing him to cry out, but stopped just short of breaking the skin and swirled my tongue around, tasting him, wanting all of him. There would be no warmup this time, no foreplay, but his cock was achingly hard and heavy in my palm, and I knew he needed this as much as I did. I worked him with my hand, swallowing his moans as I kissed him, driving my tongue into his mouth. Tracing a vein on his cock with my thumb, I then ran my thumb over the head, wetting it with his precum and groaning with him.

"I can't wait," I muttered, standing and letting Jacob slide off my lap, keeping hold of him until he was steady on his feet, and giving him only a second before I pushed him onto the couch, bending him over the back and kneeling on the cushion behind him. Jacob dug in between the couch cushions—apparently, he had planned for this—and knew me well enough that I would be on the edge of control. I snatched the bottle of lube from his palm as he offered it to me, and squirting a generous amount onto my hand, and I palmed my cock, the wet sounds making Jacob shudder. Using my lubed fingers, I pressed two inside him, working them around, getting him ready for me. Growling, I then gripped his hips. He should be thankful for small mercies. My eyes were changing to yellow as the scent of his arousal mingled with mine, while the combined scents of our bonding permeated the air until my instinct to claim was triggered.

Lining my cock up at his entrance, I pushed forward *hard,* and Jacob cried out, gripping the couch. I pushed until I was seated all the way inside him and stilled for only a moment.

My jaw twitched. "Are you okay?"

Jacob nodded against the couch, adjusting his position so he was bent a little bit further, offering himself to me. "Yes. Take me."

Leaning over him, I wrapped my arm around his body and grabbed his cock, hissing into his ear as I thrust in and out of his ass. "Lose control with me."

Jacob moaned, and I gripped him harder, pushing him past his limit. He gripped my cock and tightened around me as his peak drew closer. The sounds he was making with every thrust—*fuck*—he was driving me crazy, and I was growling against his neck, the growls turning into snarls as I came closer.

With a groan, I came, continuing to thrust hard into him as he came in my hand and over the couch, working him and drawing out his orgasm.

Jacob squeezed his eyes shut, and when he opened them, they were a blazing yellow.

But he wasn't a monster, he was simply Jacob.

My Jacob.

Mine.

So, what does a demon do when they leave Hell and plan on living it up on Earth?

Anything they want.

But for me, it all came down to this.

Finding the one I wanted to be with, creating a bond I never intended to sever. Then spending the rest of our days knowing that when we come back home to our shared apartment, we've got all night, and if we fancy, all the next day, to be nowhere but together.

God's greatest gift—*fucking.*

Jacob, my love, my bonded partner, for as long as I am still breathing.

No one else will do.

He is the human in me, and I, the demon in him.

ACKNOWLEDGMENTS

Wow. Just wow.

The sixth and final book in the *Unearthly Sins* novels. I'm lost for words, and those who know me know how incredibly out of character that is.

First of all, I will say this—this is not the end of the *Sins* novels. There are other series to come, so do not despair, dear reader!

As with everything I write, these novels are my heart and soul on paper. When I said I'll miss these characters, I meant that in a completely visceral way. I feel the same sort of grief after I finish reading a series I love or watching a television show or movie. I get attached easily and throw myself one hundred percent into the stories I write, as well as the ones I enjoy in other mediums. So I'll grieve for these characters because it'll be like missing a part of myself.

Is that weird? I can't even tell anymore. I think I've reached a new level of weirdness. But hey, I've chosen to embrace it.

I can't thank my team and friends enough who helped me along the way with my writing and publishing journey with their general support and, of course, their knowledge, expertise, and all that good stuff we need to help us succeed. I'm certain without them, I'd still be floundering around with an unedited manuscript, uncertain of what step to take next.

In no particular order—Chris, Kate, Kay, Kimberly, Ashleigh, Kathy, and Andrea.

And my parents, of course. My mother insists on owning all the paperbacks to see them on her shelf. Sweet, right? But not her type of books, and I get that.

Mum, if you ever do read them, just skip over *those* scenes, okay? For both our sakes.

And, of course, Jason, for whom mere words are never enough to express how much you mean to me and how much I appreciate your constant support and encouragement. I mean it when I say I wouldn't be the person I am today without you.

So, where to now? There are other *Sins* novels to explore. We certainly need to follow Cole and find out what that man is up to. And what about Bane and Dante? I've had questions about them, and yes, the Hellhound Sins is a plan too. Am I giving too much away? I don't think so. Think of it as a special tidbit for reading this far into my self-indulgent ramblings known as the acknowledgment section. I have many, many plans to put words on paper and bring them to you because if I don't get these stories out of my head, I don't know what I'll do.

And aliens.

I'm not saying there'll be aliens, but there will be aliens.

Looking for sexy aliens with giant c*cks? Stick with me.

So, thank you for reading and sharing this journey with me. I honestly hope these stories stay with you as they will with me and that you love the characters just as much. Authors need our readers, and we appreciate you. We really do. Every single one of you.

Love it? Please leave a review.

Because we're needy, us authors, and we crave constant validation.

And Frank, my demon Dom and the first *Sins* character to stroll into my mind, I think I'll miss you most of all.

You and Mike, though, you'll take care of each other. I know it.

ANGELS AND FIRE BOOKS
Find our exciting stories at:
www.angelsandfirebooks.com.au

READER GROUP

Want access to fun, prizes and sneak peeks?
Join my Facebook Reader Group.
https://www.facebook.com/groups/588038442170571

NEWSLETTER

Sign up for my Newsletter.
https://www.subscribepage.com/angelsandfirebooks

BOOKBUB

https://www.bookbub.com/authors/stefanie-dawn

GOODREADS

Add my books to your TBR list
on my Goodreads profile.
https://www.goodreads.com/author/
show/21761217.Stefanie_Dawn

AMAZON

https://www.amazon.com/author/stefaniedawn

WEBSITE

http://www.angelsandfirebooks.com.au/

INSTAGRAM

https://www.instagram.com/angelsandfirebooks

EMAIL

info@angelsandfirebooks.com.au

FACEBOOK

https://www.facebook.com/stefaniedawnwriter

About THE AUTHOR

Stefanie Dawn has been a writer and creative soul all her life **and** strives to give her readers stories they can escape into as they become absorbed in the worlds created.

When she isn't writing, Stefanie might be painting, reading, or watching movies. She loves the process of producing films as another form of storytelling. There's also a good chance she'll be baking some delicious treats—pretending she won't later regret consuming them—or simply enjoying a cocktail with friends.

Stefanie Dawn lives in South Australia with her ever-supportive partner and a lovable gang of rescue cats.

You can stay up to date with
Stefanie and her books at:
www.angelsandfirebooks.com.au